"O Thiam Chin is a writer at the height of his powers."
—Stephanie Ye, author of *The Billion Shop*

"O shows his ability to get to the heart of his characters and to make us care as each new layer of their experience is revealed."
—*Singapore Poetry*

"Nuanced and powerful, elegiac accounts of the failings and frustrations of love."
—*The Business Times* on *Now That It's Over* (EBFP 2015 Winner)

"There have been many novels about natural catastrophe and the tragedies that it engenders, but *Now That It's Over* is refreshing in its portrayal of destruction of the worst kind—self-destruction. The two couples are dissatisfied with the mundane emptiness in their lives and it is only through an act of god that some of them manage to move forward, the novelist ably illustrating the tragedy of suffering an emotional tsunami; battered by waves of insecurity, deceit and misunderstanding."
—*Mackerel*

"O Thiam Chin whips solid ground from beneath one's feet. He seems resolute in gesturing towards forces that lie beyond our domestic lives and Singapore's insular, urban environs."
—Laura Kho, The Arts House

FOX FIRE GIRL

FOX FIRE GIRL

A NOVEL

O THIAM CHIN

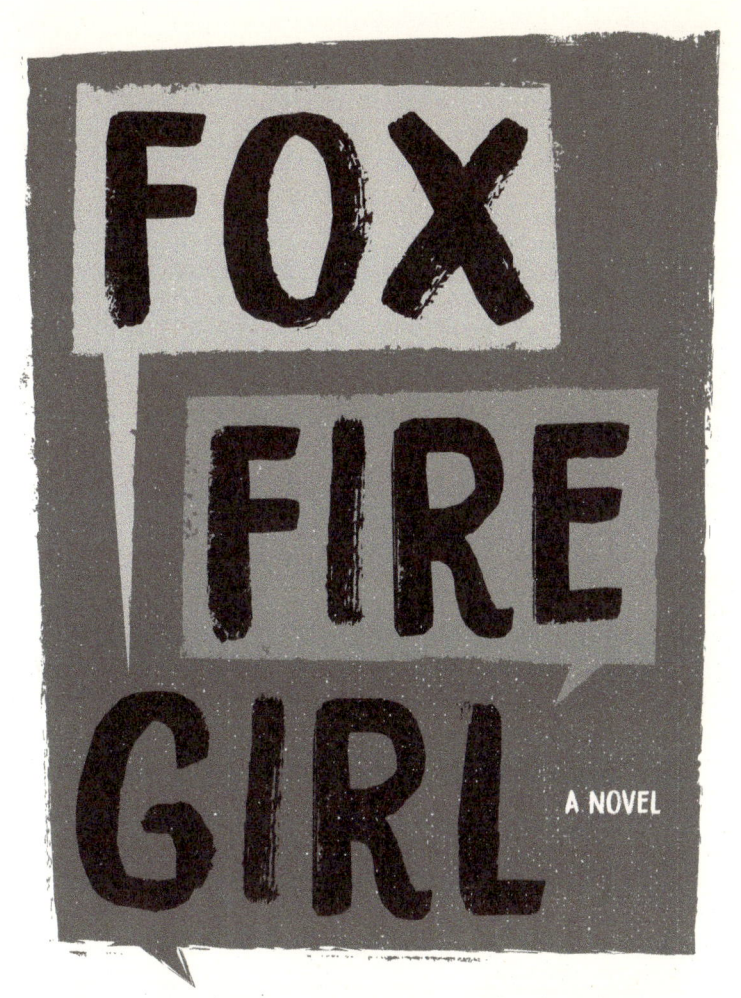

EPIGRAM BOOKS
SINGAPORE · LONDON

EPIGRAM BOOKS UK
FIRST PUBLISHED IN 2017 BY EPIGRAM BOOKS SINGAPORE
THIS EDITION PUBLISHED IN GREAT BRITAIN IN MAY 2018
BY EPIGRAM BOOKS UK

COPYRIGHT © 2017 BY O THIAM CHIN
AUTHOR PHOTO BY ALLAN SIEW. USED WITH PERMISSION.

THE MORAL RIGHT OF THE AUTHOR HAS BEEN ASSERTED.

ALL CHARACTERS AND EVENTS IN THIS PUBLICATION, OTHER THAN THOSE CLEARLY IN THE PUBLIC DOMAIN, ARE FICTITIOUS AND ANY RESEMBLANCE TO REAL PERSONS, LIVING OR DEAD, IS PURELY COINCIDENTAL.

ALL RIGHTS RESERVED. NO PART OF THIS BOOK MAY BE REPRODUCED, STORED IN A RETRIEVAL SYSTEM, OR TRANSMITTED BY ANY FORM OR BY ANY MEANS, MECHANICAL, PHOTOCOPYING, RECORDING OR OTHERWISE, WITHOUT THE PRIOR PERMISSION IN WRITING OF THE PUBLISHER.

A CIP CATALOGUE RECORD FOR THIS BOOK IS
AVAILABLE FROM THE BRITISH LIBRARY.

ISBN   978-1-91-209864-4

PRINTED AND BOUND IN   GREAT BRITAIN BY CLAYS LTD, ST IVES PLC
                                   EPIGRAM BOOKS UK
                                   55 BAKER STREET
                                   LONDON, W1U 7EU

---

10 9 8 7 6 5 4 3 2 1

WWW.EPIGRAMBOOKS.UK

FOR YVONNE LEE

FOX

BEFORE YIFAN CAME back into my life, and before I knew about her true identity, I had tried to take my life but failed. I had broken up with her six months before then, for reasons I could no longer remember clearly. After I saw her at the hospital that day, she suddenly waltzed back into my life, front and centre, as if nothing had changed since we parted.

We had dated for a few months, a haze of days. What had I remembered from that earlier, short-lived relationship? Not much, to be frank, except for the intense petty quarrels and the sex. And also the long pockets of silence we kept up till one of us eventually relented. There was only so much we could bear before something finally went south, turned bitter. But this was my side of the story, and we know there's always another side. Maybe even more than one.

The thing was, I liked Yifan a lot when I first knew her, and the attraction was mutual. But those initial feelings ran a short course and then expired. There wasn't enough in the relationship to sustain it, to keep it afloat, though we kept at it, pushing along dutifully like two shipwrecked survivors in a lifeboat heading nowhere. It was futile, hopeless even. And so when the right time opened up—was there ever a right or good time for a break-up?—Yifan initiated the end, and I found myself going along with the decision, not really caring one way or another.

But that felt like a long time ago, a story taken from a different life.

Nothing seemed to have changed for Yifan when I bumped into her at the hospital. Small of frame with a round, severe face, she looked a few years younger than she actually was—twenty-four, twenty-five? She had called out to me then—her voice ringing out, pulling me towards her—and later put her hand on mine, smiling, all teeth, inscrutable. We chatted for some time—mostly she talked and I listened—and that afternoon was the start of something new between us.

Yet the past was never far away, sticking to us even when we began anew: a tiny seed falling from an old tree onto the same earth, blooming with new shoots and complicated roots. We brought our past into the present, like long shadows trailing us, and there was no way to escape this. What was Yifan's past? Where had she been in the six months we were apart; what had she been doing? I was curious, naturally, and part of my curiosity was motivated by my own guilt—was she still angry over the last break-up? Did she feel unjustly treated? Nothing in her current actions or behaviours told me otherwise, and yet something continued to eat at me. As if sensing my thoughts, Yifan chose to remain mum on this, as if the past did not matter to her any more, a thing to be discarded and forgotten entirely. Yet the past had its way of eluding us, to throw us off its scent, before it finally caught up.

What I remember most vividly: Yifan's unshakeable presence at the hospital, three months ago. I had just been discharged, a week after being admitted for my suicide attempt, still groggy from the meds and too much sleep, my mind cottony and half-gone; then there she was, a shard of light. Like I said, we chatted. And then, as if it were the most natural of things, the next step in the sequence of events, she came back to my flat and we had sex. I had not felt any sexual desire for some time, but when she led me by hand into my bedroom and onto my bed, I fell right into it unthinkingly. She steered me along, move by move, and it was as if nothing had changed since we last broke up, every act deeply familiar, every touch a memory pulled from our bones.

Nothing had prepared me for the renewed urgency of the desire that sprang out of nowhere from my own broken body after this fateful session. Whenever we made love, it would feel like I'd been given another chance to regain myself, to reach for something that had been lost to me. I leapt at every opportunity, and I was relieved to find Yifan returning my enthusiasm in her own ways. My recovery was slow and long-drawn—the cut was deep—but the sex we had was something I looked forward to, an absolution, a necessary part of my life. Though I never told Yifan of this need, I could sense she was aware of it, and was willing to accommodate it. But there was a catch. Yifan wanted something in return: for me to read her a story after we had sex.

I like stories, she told me. *I like to hear them, and you're a writer; you have plenty of stories.*

What was there to lose? I'd simply trade one thing for another, no complication, no questions.

She did not mind whether I read an old story or something I was working on at the time, and she wasn't particular about the type of story it was either. She would still give it her full attention. The tilt and angle of her head on my chest as she listened, her even breathing, the stillness of her body—what did she hear? How did my words enter her? As mere vibrations across her skin, perhaps, reaching her inner ear? Fully absorbed, Yifan fell still as an animal in hibernation. Sometimes I'd think she had fallen asleep, but in the next moment she would tilt her head upwards as if she had picked up some disturbance in the air.

Even after weeks of reading to her, I still did not know how she felt about any of my stories. Although she would shake her head, sigh or laugh at certain parts, she never offered a word or comment. Did she even like them? What was she looking for? In her still, quiet presence, I took my time with the stories, pausing to consider every new word or sentence, making minor adjustments as I proceeded. The story changed as I read it, taking a turn here, making a stop there, diverting into unknown paths away from its original design. It was a strange experience to see a story, fixed and autonomous on a page, living a different existence as the words left my tongue and left their mark in the ears of another. How many lives does one story lead—one in many, or perhaps many stories in a single, larger existence? What shapes did the story take in Yifan's mind—and what did she make of it?

Whatever the case, Yifan listened to the stories with her undivided attention, rapt and enthralled, like a child spellbound by a new magic trick. And the spell worked on us both: her with her immersion in the storytelling, and me with my need to keep her beside me. But no story was ever long enough to hold the spell through the night. I might cheat at the ending, prolonging the inevitable or stretching the outcomes, but sooner or later the words would run out. I dreaded this final moment, for it meant that Yifan would stir from her reverie, move away, put on her clothes and prepare to leave. I wouldn't be able to stop her, not even with a desperate offer to tell her another story.

One is enough, she would say, turning a kind gaze at me.

When Yifan first came into my life, I was still trying to sort it out—drinking too much, occasional party drugs, a long sterile period of not writing, and the return of depression. I could not recall much of what she had told me about her life except a few sketchy details: she was from Ipoh ("Some kampung at the outskirts of the state, you won't know where it is even if I tell you") and had been working as a waitress in a seafood restaurant since she came to Singapore ("You take the orders, pass them along to the kitchen, and serve; it's not that hard, really, so what's not to like about it?"). I vaguely remembered sending her home once or twice—she lived in the same estate as me, somewhere in the eastern side of Ang Mo Kio—though if you were to ask me where exactly, I'd be hard-pressed to give you an answer. Still the mind turned up odd surprises now and then, dredging up old memories when I least expected it; a word or turn of phrase from Yifan and a new plane of images, full and unbroken, would surface in my head. Yes, I still remembered that and no, it should be as it was.

Memories of her might have stayed hidden but irrevocable within me, but what parts of Yifan remained the same? And what changed all the time? Every time I looked at her, I had a sense of something constantly in flux, changing as the light fell on her at different hours, as if she were trying to work out the shape and intent of who she was. But did I know enough about her to form this impression? I had barely had a grip over my own thoughts.

Still, what little I remembered fed an insatiable need for more. I needed to know everything about her. And so I persisted, masking my compulsion with feigned, innocuous curiosity. Eventually I was able to form a clearer picture of Yifan's family and background. She was the youngest in a family of nine kids: six brothers, two sisters. Her parents had worked on a fruit plantation in Ipoh that grew pomelos and durians for nearly 40 years before retiring. As a child Yifan had helped out in the plantation along with four elder brothers, and whatever she earned went into her parents' pockets. She had come to Singapore to work because she wanted to get away from her family.

I turned these hard little kernels of facts into pieces I could use to put together an image of her in my head. I needed this full, unobscured image of Yifan to hold myself together, to know that I had not conjured her up in the well of my loneliness. Because if she existed, then I too existed. There had been days—lying on the bed in the hospital, and waking up at the table after a night of writing—that I had felt like nothing more than a wisp of a figure; closer to death than life, the feeling so unbearable that I wished I had cut a bit deeper in my last attempt to erase myself. But I had survived—panicking enough when I saw the blood to make the emergency call—and now what was left was to take it a day at a time, moment by moment. Hardly an existence, but still.

Because we did not have any sort of arrangement, I could never tell when Yifan would appear at my doorstep. She would come over slightly past 11pm, after knocking off from work, and would stay till I finished telling her a story after we had sex. When she left—she had not spent a full night at my place so far—I would lie on the bed, trying to work out my thoughts as I recalled the smell of her body on my fingers. On most nights, she would bring over the leftovers from the restaurant where she worked— fried spring chicken or prawn rolls— and we would eat at the coffee table in the living room. If I wasn't hungry, she would put the food away in the fridge, and I'd microwave it for the next day's meals. She occasionally bought Tiger beer, which we took turns drinking straight from the bottle. I liked how the beer flushed Yifan's cheeks and neck, giving her a sharper, more beguiling allure; when I touched her in bed later, her skin would radiate a smooth, delicate heat. When we were done eating and drinking, Yifan would clear everything away, then take a quick shower. I didn't mind the greasy, smoky smell that clung to her after a day of work, but Yifan was too self-conscious about her personal hygiene to ignore it.

Once a week, she would come over to my flat with a bag filled with fruits, biscuits, canned sardines and luncheon meat, packs of instant ramen and Nescafé coffee, and cook a meal to share. I had taken over the flat after my parents passed away when I was in my late twenties; I was never close to them, unlike my elder brother, who took care of them when they fell to their respective illnesses, lung cancer and heart disease. Sometimes, Yifan would clean up the flat despite my protests. The only things she left untouched while cleaning were my books and papers, which were scattered all over the dining table and coffee table in the living room. She would occasionally pick up a sheaf of paper and give it a quick scan. Yifan had had to drop out of secondary school, though she didn't give any reason, and I'd wonder how much she understood from these cursory glances. In any case, I didn't make any attempt to hide my writings from her.

If I remembered anything about our lovemaking from our earlier relationship, it was all lost in these new sessions which were, by all measures, intense, fervid, consuming. It also didn't help that back then I was having sex with other women, something I took great effort to hide from her. Now that shred of my life seemed a long time ago, lived by someone I barely knew, and I felt very little remorse in discarding it. Yifan never brought up our previous relationship, and I knew enough to do the same. What was past was past, and we were starting anew.

In my idle moments, I imagined the sex we once had and tried to compare it to the present, even though the details were sketchy. How much did the body remember over time—the odd angle of Yifan's arm, the curve of her back as she took me in? The past colliding with the present, churning the same actions into similar images, bleeding into one another—did she always throw her head back as she came? Had I always taken her nipple into my mouth like this, flicking the hardening tip with my tongue? Did I remember everything correctly?

The first few times we made love after reconnecting, the

whole thing had felt procedural, a step-by-step sequence leading to a climax. We were gentle and careful to a fault, as if we were both scared of making the wrong move, of acting out of sync. Yifan led the way mostly, guiding our bodies through the different stages and positions. I felt her eyes on me, watching how I responded to her and making small calculations, minor adjustments. It would have been all too mechanical if not for the fleeting streaks of pleasure I saw sweeping across Yifan's face from time to time, the suppressed groans escaping her wet parted lips. I wanted to feel her intensity, her pleasure in what we were doing, and in some imperceptible ways I did: my skin flipped inside out, no longer a barrier, but a flimsy membrane through which everything seeped to fill me. I felt tethered to Yifan through her skin, by her breath. Somehow, I knew she had needed this too, for reasons of her own.

After we had sex I'd turn to the side table, pick up the story or book and begin to read. Our bodies still damp and musky, slowly losing their tension, Yifan would lean into my chest, breathing lightly on my skin. I had always liked this transition between our lovemaking and the storytelling for its uncomplicated nature—the unambiguous moment when it crossed from one threshold to another. She needed a story, and I needed a listener. When I was done reading, there would be a skip of time where we would lie very still in bed, our bodies tangled up and our minds in separate spheres of thought, before Yifan got out of bed and put on her clothes, turning her back towards me. Before she left, Yifan would give me a kiss on the cheek and remind me about the leftovers in the fridge.

Once, I stepped outside after she left and leant against the railing along the corridor to have a smoke. I watched as she emerged from the void deck of my block and walked the path that cut across a dark field, dissolving into shadows under the dim yellow light of the streetlamps. She always seemed in a hurry to leave. I finished the cigarette and returned to the flat, killing all the lights save the one in the kitchen. There I made a pot of coffee and lit another Pall Mall, watching the pale fingers of smoke spiral and disappear into the air. After a while, I brought out my laptop from the study room and, while waiting for the kettle to whistle, opened the new story I had just read to Yifan and started revising it. The cup of Nescafé coffee I made later was left almost entirely untouched as I worked on the story, the air in the kitchen growing dense with cigarette smoke. When I was finished, I took a final sip of coffee and poured the rest into the sink.

That night, I was unable to sleep, my mind clogged with

a swarm of thoughts. I went back into the kitchen, wet a rag and started cleaning the stove, the kitchen table, the shelves. Afterwards I sat at the kitchen table and smoked, waiting for my body to signal its fatigue. A reel of images and words pinwheeled through my head, held together by its own logic. With all the windows shut, I listened to the flat's silence. A scene floated into my mind, unprompted: the phone in my bloodied hand, crackling with static, the overhead lights of the kitchen blazing. The sonorous voice of the operator ringing in my ears: *stay calm, is anyone with you now?* The blood that never seemed to stop, pouring from the dark slit in my wrist. The pain was there, momentarily, in the first insertion and the cut—and then it was gone, and all I could hear was a wave of silence: the black dogs had stopped their howling, their hunger appeased. How long they had hounded me—prancing and watching at the borders, waiting for my next move, anticipating my fall.

I closed my eyes and wiped the scene from my mind.

Yet the black dogs were still there; I could feel their presence, their shadows stretching over my life. How long could I hold up before they came for me again? Was madness a slow progression, or a sudden fall?

I had always suffered from these dark spells since I was a child—extended periods when my mind would spiral into free fall, and every thought I had was a thought that reached for some kind of oblivion, for the relief of death. They came to me, quietly and unannounced, and then they stayed. Days that I couldn't get out of bed, let alone eat or sleep, days that felt like the longest days ever, each second beating its own deadly knell. When I was 18, my parents sent me to a doctor who sent me to a psychiatrist who dispatched me for two months to Woodbridge Hospital. I took all the pills, and I listened to all the advice: *go out, make more friends, get some sunlight, take up a sport, smile more.* I tried, I did everything I was told, and I had good days. My parents were pleased.

And then the dogs would appear again, snapping at my heels.

My father: *Why are you doing this to yourself? Why are you doing this to us?*

My mother: *Can't you try harder? You know you can overcome this if you want to. You only need to want it.*

My brother: *Don't be weak, you're a fucking man. Don't give in just like that.*

And so I tried. I kept the black dogs at bay, I left them cold and starving. I saw another psychiatrist, I took the new drugs. I met new people, new faces. I dated and I had sex and I felt positive. I learnt to write fiction, and the words became a weapon and a shield that I used to defend myself; the stories were maps to plot my escape. I built up an arsenal of words; I wrote story after story. The world grew inside me, now a fortress, now a city: I had my control, my authority, the light pouring in and flooding every corner. I felt good about myself for the first time in my life.

And then my parents died, one six months after the other.

Still I held up for a while, for four, five months. Then, without any warning, the dogs came back. The days stretched bleakly on in a long bated breath, a seam of time without end, unfurling inside me, feathers like razors, cutting.

What if I had died the last time—would it have mattered to anyone? I no longer stayed in touch with my older brother after my parents' deaths; we had our own lives and we lived with the decisions we made. I had enjoyed solitude from a young age and long grew used to being alone. I managed life on my own terms, living with very little, and expecting even less from other people. People are needy and demanding and they will never be able to help themselves, I often reminded myself. I did not feel the need to impose myself on others, and likewise, I refused to be burdened by others. I would die, and there would be no one to mourn for me, and it would not be a terrible thing.

But with Yifan I had doubts. I knew I had leant too

heavily on her, and the gaping pit inside me was widening and deepening over time. When I was with her I felt the pangs of my own loneliness more intensely, and I was suddenly afraid of my urgent, desperate need, and where it would lead me eventually.

Yet for the first time in a very long while my days were filled not with fear or encroaching darkness, but with a small sense of wonder, even possibilities.

• • •

"Derrick, I'm not what you think I am," Yifan said, after we had been seeing each other for four months. "I take different forms, different disguises, and this is just one of them."

I turned to look at Yifan when she said this. With her head on my chest, and her words flitting across my skin, I thought, for a moment, that I had heard something else. I had just finished telling her a new story, one about a young woman who had to take care of her late father's cat. Yifan had liked the story, judging from her nodding throughout the reading.

"I'm much older than I look. I have lived for so long that the days or years no longer matter to me. Not in the way that they matter to you," Yifan said, lowering her voice, keeping it soft, steely.

"I don't understand."

"It's okay. You won't understand unless I tell you. I'm a fox spirit."

With that, Yifan got out of bed, put on her clothes, and left the flat quietly.

For the rest of the night, I found myself in a state of restlessness and, not knowing what to do, went around the flat, cleaning and wiping and washing, unable to keep my thoughts in order. Even when I closed my eyes, trying to catch some sleep, my mind refused to shut down. I smoked and drank coffee to pass the long hours, waiting for the morning light to break through the night.

Yifan texted me the following day and came over late at night with a bag of supper: seafood fried rice and stir-fried kailan. Over the meal, she did not bring up anything about being a fox spirit, and I wondered if I had imagined what she had said. *I'm coming unhinged*, I thought. We ate supper in silence.

Then, later, after we had sex, Yifan continued her story.

"I was ten when I first started noticing the changes to my body, small signs that told me I was different from other people. I was so scared by the transformation—the tail, my canine teeth, the appetite. I thought I was a monster, until my parents assured me. They knew I would realise this sooner or later, having come to this stage of maturity. They were ready to tell me everything about our identity. They wanted me to know what, or who, I am."

"So your whole family—are they all fox spirits?"

"Yes, all of us. We have been around for a long time."

"How long?"

"Long enough to see people come and go, to see countries rise and fall, to see wars and battles and floods. The harvests and the passing of seasons. My parents were born in Gansu, China, in the eighth century, and they settled in Malaysia at the turn of the last century. They felt it was better in Malaysia after the famine and constant upheavals in their hometown. They wanted an unobtrusive, quieter life."

"But then why did you leave your family?"

"Why? Why do we leave what's so familiar to us? Simple. We leave because we want a different kind of life. I left because I needed to." Yifan drew away from me, her gaze moving inwards.

"Don't you miss your family?" I ventured again, my voice subdued.

"Sometimes, but I've gotten used to it. The thing is, I can sense my family through my body, no matter how far I am from them. I can feel them right in my flesh, a unique sensation for each one of them. My parents, each of my siblings. I can feel their pulse in me, as if their hearts are right beside mine. I know how each of them is doing from different parts of my body.

"Once, I felt a sharp jab of pain on the right side of my lower abdomen, and I knew something bad had happened to my third elder brother. I could feel his heartbeats getting weaker, and it was a terrible, awful feeling: I could feel his life leaving me, and there was nothing I could do about it. The sharp pain ended after some time, and there was this strange hollowness in place of it, a vast emptiness.

"Later, I found out from my mother that my brother had been killed by loan sharks over a gambling debt. He bled to death after they stabbed him in the chest. It was so sudden that none of us had a chance to come to his rescue.

"The place where my elder brother used to live inside me remains dark and hollow, even now."

. . .

The first man Yifan fell in love with was someone who worked in a provision shop in the kampung where her family lived. She was 15, quiet and introverted, and had noticed the young man when she was helping her parents make the runs to the shop, picking up groceries or buying the nightly Chinese newspaper. The man, bespectacled and sinewy, was the shop assistant—the middle son of the shop owner—and had been working there since completing secondary school, at the same school that Yifan attended. They had been in each other's orbit for a long time—they were both born in the same kampung in Ipoh and had never left the state in their lives, not even for a short holiday. Growing up, they were friendly but not close. He was there all the time, Yifan explained, and then something happened—a shift of perception, the tide of inexplicable feelings—and she could not stop noticing him.

When this happened, Yifan found herself paying close attention to his clothes and gestures and tics, musing contemplatively over his words from the brief conversations they had. Something grew and gnawed inside her—a wild, unwieldy feeling that had seemed like a physical pain; to be near him felt like an ordeal, as if she were treading on thin ice, waiting to fall through. On the surface nothing had changed between them, but the change inside her had irreversibly split her into two distinct irreconcilable states, like night and day, air and water.

Naturally, Yifan told nothing of this to her parents or siblings; it was something she was still unable to put into words or make any sense of. She nursed her infatuation for the man quietly, privately, and her feelings grew in accordance.

Then one day, Yifan did the inevitable—she made the first move. She did not approach him or talk to him; instead she followed him. At that point in her life, four years after discovering her true nature, she had learnt how to transform herself, though her abilities were weak and limited. A sparrow, a mouse, a house lizard—these transformations could be achieved with some practice. She would throw her whole being into an image of an animal in her mind, and then she would physically become the creature. It took a long time before she even got round the idea of the transformation—losing the particularity of her physical self, yet still retaining her sense of self and her thoughts in the mind of the beast she was impersonating. *It is an odd feeling, to live in a completely different body, to be that very thing I imagined*, Yifan said. Every transformation was a novel experience, and each one would take its own toll, something she only realised much later.

The first time she decided to follow the young man, she transformed herself into a sparrow. By then, she had been observing him from a distance for weeks, and was well aware of his daily routine, the cycles of his life. At 4.30

in the afternoon, he left the shop for his usual half-hour break, carrying a bag of sunflower seeds. Yifan, as a sparrow, followed him to a clearing under a large casuarina tree, a short distance from the back of the provision shop. Often he would head there for a short nap or to daydream on a wooden bench he had constructed out of a few old planks. The shade provided by the tight canopy of branches was gentle and cooling, and the occasional breeze had a soothing, calming effect on the mind. There was no one around; the silence was punctured only by the shuffling of the leaves and the persistent droning of the crickets. Yifan stayed on a low branch of a nearby tree, keeping her gaze on him, her heart pounding madly in her newly constricted chest. The young man remained quiet as he sat on the wooden bench.

After staring into the field of lalang for some time, the man untied the knot on the bag of sunflower seeds and reached in for a handful, scattering them on the ground before him. Two stray chickens, plump with luscious brown feathers, crept towards the seeds, pecking at the sand. The man watched them studiously. Yifan came closer, skipping to a branch that overlooked the arc of the man's back. Had she made the slightest sound, a chirp, he would have noticed her. Being so close to him set her body thrumming with a deep excitement. She was barely able to hold everything inside the tiny form she inhabited.

The man lay back and stretched himself out, taking up the full length of the bench. He looked up into the overlapping branches, his left hand blocking out the light. Had he seen her, she wondered? Her heart leapt into her beak, and she broke out into a barely suppressed twitter despite intending to keep herself hidden. Then she froze—the body was still new to her, with its strange little tics—her head cocked at a slight angle. She could feel the man's curious gaze on her; the sudden awareness was a heavy cloak that held her immobile. The man sent up a whistle, smiling. Yifan did not dare to look down, or do anything.

After what seemed like an immeasurably long time, she peeked down and saw that the man had closed his eyes. He had fallen asleep. From her perch, Yifan studied the man's features—the fringe of hair that fell across his forehead, his loose, full lips, the delicate line of his ears. She had never had the chance to look at him so closely—there was always an impulse to pull away, to lower her eyes, by her own volition—and now that she had been presented with one, she felt at a loss. What did she want from all this? What was she hoping to get from him—a reciprocation of feelings? Or something else entirely, something she had yet to come around to—a deep yearning, or a dark urge, perhaps?

She flapped her wings tentatively, then flew down to the edge of the bench. Deep in sleep, the man's hands had dropped to his sides, extending to the ground. Up close, Yifan felt the soft heat emanating from his body, a warm invisible skin wrapped all around him. The sounds of the surrounding forest came to Yifan as if from a different age, from a time fractured from reality—discordant, shrouded, tempestuous. What was he dreaming, if he was dreaming?

She came as close as she could, never lifting her eyes from him. Yifan was breathless with the possibilities running through her head. She had wanted to return to her human form there and then, but it would have been unthinkable. So she perched there, silently and stolidly, and bade her time, observing him and restraining her thoughts.

Around them, the world throbbed and pulsated with strong, stubborn beats. A deeply magical place, full of air and light.

• • •

This went on for two weeks before Yifan discovered something about the young man. During one of her observations, she heard him—or rather she felt his thoughts, as if he had spoken them aloud. She had discovered this while she was spying on him in his room at night, in the disguise of a house lizard. There was a sudden interruption in the flow of her thoughts, as if something had barged into her consciousness. At first, she brushed the mental nudge aside, and then in the flicker of realisation, she knew it was something from outside of her, that it had come from the man.

"It was like he was speaking directly to me," Yifan said. "But not in words, or anything that could be put into words."

"Not in words?"

"No. Only the shape of his thought, but it was enough. I could sense its weight and outline inside me, and I could make out what he was thinking. It's like how you know a chair is a chair in the dark—you recognise its form when you run your hands over it. It was a frightening thing."

"Frightening?"

"To have a small access into his mind, or anyone's mind—to really know someone from his core, how he thinks or feels… It's just…"

Yifan closed her eyes, taking a deep breath. She moved her fingers across my chest, as if tracing some invisible script across my skin.

"That first time, I held on to his thought for very long.

It took a while to fully form in my head, and I was very careful not to disturb it lest it disappear. It was my first experience of hearing someone's thoughts, and I wanted it to last as long as it could. The thought itself was mundane—something about clearing out part of a storeroom for new stocks the next day. But it was a secret knowledge of his life that had been revealed only to me. Only I had been given a glimpse into its workings. I was so scared of being discovered that I just let the thought sit in me until it faded away.

"After this happened, I became very restless, unable to keep myself from fretting all the time. I still helped my father with deliveries to the provision shop where he worked. But when our eyes met, I would quickly glance away, afraid he could sense what I could do.

"I still held on to the images of his thought in my head, though they became more vague every time I dredged them up, as if their imprints were slowly being wiped away. I was terribly afraid of losing the thought altogether. I wanted more—I needed to know more. I wanted to get inside him, into his head. This idea gave me such a thrill that I could barely think of anything else. I knew it could happen again. And of course it did, not long after."

• • •

A week later, Yifan took the form of a moth and went to the man late at night. He lived in a room at the back of the shop, a dingy place that only had space for a single bed, a chair, and a wire clothesline. It was just past one and the man was still awake, lying on the thin mattress. Yifan stationed herself on the wall, hiding in the shadow. The man had cast only a brief glance at her when she flew in through the open window, before turning back to stare at the ceiling, where a single light bulb hung from a wire cable. Weak, yellow light saturated the room.

Gliding down, Yifan came closer to the man, keeping herself motionless on the edge of his chair. Soon enough, she felt a nudge in her head—one light push and a stray thought rose forth. She steadied herself against the surge of feelings rippling through her.

And then an odd thing happened: barely had she grasped the form and contents of the man's thought—something from a sketch comedy he had seen on TV that night—that she was nudged by another thought. It hit her suddenly that she was reading his mind. The man's thoughts snuck in and slipped through her mind as if the latter had suddenly become porous. *Don't lose your mind*, she told herself. *Hold on, hold on.*

As she came around to the idea, Yifan was able to get a better grip of the man's thoughts. Each thought generated a rush of images before dissolving, followed swiftly by another thought and its cluster of images. Some of the man's thoughts were trivial, day-to-day stuff—tasks to complete, errands to run—while others were a mishmash of odds and ends cobbled together without any particular sequence or meaning. But what puzzled Yifan most were those murky, shapeless thoughts that hovered at the edge of her mind. She could not get a firm sense of what they were. If she could not read these thoughts, how about the man? Was he failing to understand his own thoughts too? She had no idea.

• • •

After Yifan started telling me about her past, I found myself unable to write. I'd turn on the laptop and stare at the blank page on the screen, not a single word or image stirring in my head. At that point, I was working on a novel about two young couples trying to find one another on a devastated island after a tsunami. But I simply could not continue the story, even though I had started with a clear direction and knew what I wanted to achieve with it. To get around this stalemate, I tried writing longhand on a notepad. I managed to scribble one sentence on the paper, but found myself revising it over and over again. Eventually I gave up and turned to the story Yifan had been telling me instead.

I wrote slowly at first, trying to distill a story from the cluster of images and impressions, careful to leave out my initial surprise and fascination. After a while, my writing picked up pace, propelling itself forward. When my back started to ache, I would stir from the writing and make more coffee or have a quick snack. I wondered where it was all going ultimately. Why had Yifan started telling me her story? And more importantly—why had I felt the need to write it all down?

My mind was racked with doubt, with questions that raised more questions. Was Yifan really a fox spirit? Could she really transform herself into an animal? And if she really could, what was I supposed to do with the knowledge? Run out and tell someone else about it? Would anyone believe me? And if the story wasn't true, was she crazy? How well did I know her after all, this woman with her irresistible hold on my life? And what could I do really—stop seeing her, and get as far away from her as possible? None of these options seemed feasible or realistic, in any case. I wanted answers—and I knew I was about to have them, soon. I just had to be patient.

As evening drew near and the flat fell into shadows, I finished up the last sentence and put away the story. I took out the leftovers from the fridge—stir-fried fish slices with ginger, and fried eggs with onions—and popped them into the microwave. I scooped out two cups of rice for the rice cooker and laid out an additional set of cutlery on the dining table.

While waiting for the rice to cook, I thought about Yifan as a moth in the man's room and the man lying on the bed, both of them thinking the same thoughts. If Yifan could read the man's thoughts, could she read mine, too? I smiled briefly at the thought of this—what did it matter? I could not stop her if she did, and if it was beyond my control, why should I care about it?

Yifan came over at 11pm, as usual. We ate the dinner that I had prepared and made aimless small talk across a range of topics: food, movies, mobile game apps. She washed up and put away the leftovers. As far as I could tell, Yifan was her usual self, affable and artless. Later, after I initiated it, we had sex. Perhaps because of what I knew, I went into the lovemaking with greater abandon. Yifan kept up her part, immersing herself fully in the act, unrestrained in her passion. When we were done, she collapsed into my arms, her body warm and flushed, covered in tiny beads of perspiration. I held her and waited for her to continue her story.

• • •

"I kept listening to his thoughts night after night. I don't think I could have stopped, and I didn't want to. There was so much I didn't know about him, and this window into his mind was all I had to peek into. I knew, in the back of my mind, that it was wrong. But I didn't care."

"He never caught on?"

"How would he know that there was someone able to read his mind? Would you believe it, if you had never heard of such things?"

"And what you were doing never bothered you at all?"

"No, not at the time. I only did what I had to do, and I wasn't thinking about what would happen next. I was in too deep to see anything else."

"You never told anyone?"

"How could I, really? Not after I found out what I could actually do. There was no turning back then."

"What do you mean?"

"A week after I realised I could hear his thoughts, I discovered something else by accident. That night, he was about to fall asleep, and just as I was about to leave, I did something out of the blue: I decided to give him a nudge by sneaking a thought into his head. It was a simple thought: *look at me.* And then, almost immediately, he scanned the room and saw me—a moth on the wall. He stared for such a long time that I wondered whether he could tell who I was. I was scared out of my wits. But of course, he couldn't have known. When he broke his stare, I flew out of the room in haste. I was shaken by the whole episode—but also secretly thrilled that he could hear me in his head. I felt overjoyed, in fact. I could finally make myself known to him.

"And then things took a different turn."

• • •

Late afternoon the following day, Yifan disguised herself as a sparrow and took up her usual spot in the tree, above the man on the bench. This time she imprinted herself right into his mind, with simple instructions: *Look up. Look at me.* The man took some time, craning his neck around. Finally he spotted Yifan in the branches, looking down at him. His face took on a slight hint of a recognition, as if he were trying to recall a distant, long-forgotten memory. Quickly, she left an image in his head: a pair of hands—hers. The man's sight turned inwards as his mind scampered after the image. She sensed his thoughts coalescing around the image she had created. She fed him more images: a bare shoulder, her legs, her peach-shaped breasts. Except her face—that she had intentionally blanked out. She animated these parts of her with delicate movements and suggestive gestures—move, arch, tremble, touch, prod, feel. She let the man's thoughts wrap themselves around hers, intertwining, amassing and building themselves up; in no time, they were thinking the same thoughts, playing the same images in their heads. Yifan could feel her heart pounding outside the tiny sparrow body she was in, as if it had been ripped out of her.

She watched as the man reached into his pants and began to tug. He had closed his eyes, deep lines at the sides of his eyes, as if in strained concentration. She watched him—from the branch and inside his head—and an intense current coursed through her senses, her body electrified from tip to tip. In her mind—and in his?—they were inseparable, united in spirit. The feeling was intolerable, yet it filled every space inside her. She had created herself in the man's mind, and he had taken her whole, without question, without resistance. In many ways, she was ecstatic beyond measure. The man had wanted every part of her.

Yet in the dark pit of her heart, she also felt a greater

sense of reality was still missing. Where was she, the real Yifan, in all this? She was, after all, merely a thought in the man's head, and this absence sat stubbornly in her, hard and intractable. She needed more—needed to fill the void, though she had no idea how to do it.

She watched as the man finally collapsed into a heap of spasms, his mind exploding in bright fragments, his thoughts scattered in torn, twisted pieces. She fled his mind like a thief taking flight, escaping into the safety of darkness.

• • •

"And I appeared to him more and more, sneaking into his mind whenever I was near him. From being inside his head, I was quite sure he didn't find anything amiss. He was completely clueless. And I knew with certainty that he had been entertaining thoughts about me the whole time. Not the real me, but the one I had created in his head. I was glad, I thought he was falling for me. But I was wrong, in the end.

"The more I entered his mind, the easier it became to influence him. I thought by giving him what he had wanted—my body, my thoughts, my love—I was securing a place for myself in his life, though I barely talked to him except for cursory greetings or a brief chat here and there. I don't think he paid any real attention to me during that time. But this didn't matter to me; I was already in his thoughts all the time. And it felt enough.

"I was so deep into what I was doing that I didn't notice what was happening to him. It was only later, when his health started to fail, that these changes became apparent to me: his gaunt face, his sunken cheeks, the void of light in his eyes. His hair turned grey overnight. I didn't link any of this to what I was doing to him, but of course, these things have their effects.

"After a while I started to get complacent and a little careless. I would leave small tracks behind in his head: a glimpse of the birthmark on my shoulder, the mole on my left cheek; little signs that would give me away. Was it intentional? I don't know. But I don't think he picked up on any of these, and if he had, it didn't register in his mind right away. As I said, I could not read some of his thoughts; those that were more ambiguous and obscure in nature. Also, I wasn't with him all day, so it was impossible to know everything that went on in his head.

"This carried on for four months, and things seemed to be going where they should. But I was wrong. I might have overlooked the changes in his appearance or behaviour, but they had already aroused the suspicions of his parents. They must have tried to find out from him what was going on, and had taken steps to help him. All I could tell was that his thoughts got slow and heavy, as if his mind had been sedated or cast down with an unseen load. Whatever they were doing—visits to the doctor or mediums, medications, talismans, pills, herbal drinks—dulled him significantly. His mind became like a swamp, thick and coagulated, barely letting in any light.

"Eventually, this came to a head so suddenly I wasn't able to do anything about it. I didn't know it would be the last time I would be in his head until it happened. That night, I was in his thoughts, and we were in the thick of the act. I was careless, and had turned my back to him for a moment. When I glanced back, I saw a look of terror on his face. Then I realised my tail was wagging wildly in the air between us. I swiftly retracted the tail, but it was too late. The man's thoughts started to run riotous, his face torn by alarm and fear. We stared at each other and I knew, without any doubt, that whatever we'd had between us was lost for good. I would not be able to get into his head anymore. He had seen through me. I exited from his head, and left quickly.

They found him in bed the next day, unconscious but still alive. When he came to, three days later, he was no longer the same: a little off in his head, they said. I didn't try to find out more, though I could not help hearing things from my parents. And although I kept my distance and my silence, I could not stop blaming myself for what had happened. I had destroyed the only good thing in my life.

"That was when I decided to leave Ipoh and head down to Singapore. I wanted to leave it all behind me. Yet I knew the consequences of my actions would stay with me for as long as I lived. But I would have to deal with it, in my own time.

"And now you know all there is to know about me, about my past. What do you want to do now?"

• • •

After Yifan left I went around the flat, restless and agitated, unable to sit or stand still even for a moment. I wondered whether I understood any of Yifan's story. The details were all there, but I did not know what to do with them. If I believed any part of it, what was next? I was at a loss. I knew I did not want to lose Yifan. But there was no guarantee, not even in the intimacy we had shared, that she would stay. Things hadn't worked out the first time. But now I had a chance to make them right.

And it boiled down to this: my decision. How quickly

life could unravel and come to naught. There for a moment, and then gone. People, loves, stories—it was only a matter of time.

Pausing under the kitchen lights, I felt a slight nudge in my mind, my thoughts pushing my consciousness towards something hidden in its crevices. How much had I lost up to now—including my grasp on my own life? I had tried to take it once and failed, and I did not have it in me to try again. Since that attempt, my existence had felt suspended, stuck in time, a pathetic figure drawn in air and shadow. What story could I make out of my life? Nothing that would matter to anyone, not even to Yifan.

And yet I had somehow found a way to live: in the stories that I had written, stories caught between life and the void, between fact and make-believe, holding up the truths that were the sum of every real or imagined thing I had felt or known or seen. These stories mattered to me. And what was Yifan's story but another way for me to get back into the flow of life? It might not be the best way to live, but it was all I had. It was sufficient—I would make it so, in time.

Taking in a deep, muddled breath, I let my thoughts settle. My mind flat-lined. Then, with a sudden flicker of shadows, I saw the moth at the edge of my vision. It had hidden itself in a dark corner of the kitchen, still and observant. For a full moment, I wondered: did it think or feel? If so, would its thoughts cross with mine, merging, taking the same path? In that instant, I saw myself as the moth—in its wings and feathered antennae, feeling its way through the long night. I could take flight any time. But instead I waited. I watched myself through the eyes of the moth, and felt my thoughts stirring alive inside its dark, cavernous mind.

Around me, the night spread its wings and darkness was upon us, full and fathomless.

FIRE

THERE WERE ONLY two things Tien Chen knew about his mother: she married his father 28 years ago, and died a week after giving birth to him. She was 30 when she died, and his father had thrown away all her photos, except two, one of which he kept in his wallet, and which had faded into a murky paleness, his mother's features barely outlined against the background. The other was framed as a portrait and placed on the altar in the living room. How they had met, and everything that happened before she died—these his father had chosen not to reveal.

From the little he knew about his parents' lives, Tien Chen pieced together a composite of their history, filled with gaps and silences. What kind of woman had his mother been? Why had she fallen in love with his father, a slight, shy man who was partially blind in the right eye? What had she seen in him? Growing up, Tien Chen tried to answer his own questions by paying close attention to what his father said and did, and attempting to form his own impressions of their past. But it had never felt sufficient.

What troubled Tien Chen was the death of his mother, something that occurred as an unfortunate result of unseen complications from a tough birth, according to his father. Tien Chen did not know whether his mother was buried or cremated; his father had never brought him to a cemetery or columbarium to pay his respects, not even during Qing Ming. It was as if his father had chosen deliberately to erase her existence, to wipe her from memory as if she had not mattered at all, a flicker of dust scattered into nothingness.

As a child, Tien Chen had felt the absence of his mother sharply, even though he had no memory of her. She was an emptiness in his head, exerting its own weight and presence. But based on what he'd gathered from his classmates' stories and accounts of their mothers, he was able to form an image of a mother he never had, one that grew more complex as he attributed more traits and features to her, willing her into existence. Sometimes, in his fervent imagining—when the figure of his mother appeared vividly alive to him—he could almost feel the reality of this person he had made up entirely in his head, a person who seemed as real to him as any other living being.

It was in such moments, or shortly after, that the ache of his loss would crush him. The made-up memories of his mother and the fact of her death—they nestled side by side in his mind like a pair of close, feuding beasts feeding on his obsession, nurtured by his deep longing. He never told anyone about these thoughts, knowing deep in his bones that it was something he had to carry alone. He often felt separated from the people around him, and nothing gave him more relief from the pressure and friction of daily life than escaping into this secret place inside him.

Yet, Tien Chen was not blind to all that his father did to make his childhood a little easier to bear. His father had allowed Tien Chen an unthinkable breadth of freedom from an age of five, just as long as he did not get into trouble, or come back home crying at every little cut or bruise. *If you want to cry then don't play,* his father would tell him, *a little pain now and then won't kill you; it might even be good for you.* Tien Chen held on to his father's words tightly, like cold, flinty stones in his palm. He bore all the pain he encountered—whether from his own carelessness or inflicted by others—with barely a whimper. He learnt ways to inure himself to it, to make himself braver than he actually was.

When he started primary school, his father gave him the keys to the flat and a weekly allowance. *You're old enough to take care of yourself now,* he'd said. As a drinks stall helper, his father clocked a 14-hour shift at a kopitiam in the housing estate where they lived, and was rarely home before ten-thirty at night. Tien Chen took to preparing his meals at home, after growing tired of eating the food from the neighbourhood kopitiams—simple-enough meals of white rice with canned luncheon meat, or instant noodles with a fried egg. Sometimes he cooked more and set aside the leftovers for his father, who would eat them cold after taking a quick shower. Tien Chen would sit at the dining table with his homework as his father ate quietly and swiftly, hardly pausing between mouthfuls. When his father asked about school, Tien Chen offered short replies with little or no elaboration that were always received with a slight nod or a blank expression. Occasionally the meals would pass with nary a word exchanged between them. This came as a relief to Tien Chen, who often worried about what he was supposed to say to his father.

Life in primary school was much tougher in ways both anticipated and unexpected. Tien Chen managed above-average grades that never called for undue attention, though he didn't like anything he was taught. What surprised him was how swiftly his classmates split into groups by interests and preferences while leaving him out completely. Shunned without any reason. He did not mind the teasing, and was more than able to fend for himself—he was tall for his age, with a stout frame, and was nimble in his movements. The girls he could safely ignore with a glare or snicker; the boys he would scuffle with in the toilet or in corners of the school field. He learnt to fight decisively—landing a well-placed punch on his opponent that cut off any potential response—to avoid prolonging these sessions. In no time, everyone was giving him a wide berth and leaving him alone. His reputation as a loner spread, and he grew gradually into this identity, carrying it with as much pride as he could muster.

Through his primary school days, Tien Chen saw the world around him as a place where he had to stay alert at all times, always aware that things could change in an instant. He had no friends, and took to his solitary state with very little fuss, a badge of unearned honour. He stayed quiet in class, keeping his eyes on the chalkboard, refusing to participate in his classmates' antics: passing little notes or comic books around, or scribbling on the back of someone's uniform. Tien Chen was rigidly attentive to whatever was happening around him, his body ready to spring into action. He sat upright, his arms on the textbook, his fingers twirling a pencil in perfect circles. He had constructed a social hierarchy of his classmates in his mind and he knew his place in it, as well as exactly who was admired or bullied or shunned. This awareness did not ruffle him, only served as a point of clarity, a useful piece of knowledge, like knowing the life-stages of a mosquito or the process of photosynthesis.

In upper primary, Tien Chen developed a keen interest in science as his innate curiosity about the natural world grew—a world which pulsated with moments of fascination and beauty for him. As a reward for scoring high marks for his science exam in Primary Four, his father bought him a thick volume, *The Big Book of Plants and Animals*. Tien Chen kept the book by his bedside and would read it every night before he slept. Taking his cue from this nightly reading, his father continued to buy books for him, first as presents, then as a fixture in his weekly expenditures. He even allowed Tien Chen to choose his own books when they were at the neighbourhood bookstore: *Electricity and Its Uses, The Key Functions of the Human Body, Rainforests of the World, The Ancient Mysteries of the Pyramids*.

Tien Chen knew how much the books cost and how they taxed his father's meagre monthly salary, yet he knew his father derived a sort of paternal pleasure—delight?—from doing something to help Tien Chen's education, and so Tien Chen did what he could to reinforce this belief. He treasured these books immensely—for they were tangible proof of his father's affection for him. Occasionally, Tien Chen would catch his father flipping through the pages while cleaning up his bedroom. His father, as far as Tien Chen was aware, only knew Chinese; he'd only attended school for a few years before leaving to work full-time to support his family. In the evenings, after dinner, Tien Chen would sit beside his father on the sofa with a book as the latter flipped through the *Lianhe Wanbao*, each comfortably and silently immersed in his own world of words and pictures.

Like any young boy, Tien Chen had his share of secrets. He loved to burn things that nobody wanted, items of little to no value. Paper, cardboard, dry leaves, branches, discarded plastic bags. He would take a box of matches from the altar in the living room and put it in his shorts pocket. Several times a day, he would reach in to finger the coarse surface of the side panel. When he was alone, he would take out a matchstick and strike it against the edge of the box, watching the maroon tip flare into a bright, noisy flame. Sometimes, he would bring the flame to the things he wanted to burn, one item at a time; occasionally, he simply watched the matchstick burn itself out, shrivelling into a black twisted shape. He liked how the flame, as if being agitated by something he could not see or feel, flickered and moved swiftly down the thin wooden sliver, the heat reaching out to bite him. He did not mind the pain—it only hurt for a brief moment.

At home, he would take whatever he wanted to burn—a torn sheaf of paper from an unused exercise book, a pizza-delivery pamphlet, an instant-noodle wrapper—to the rubbish chute in the kitchen. He would place the item on the inside of the chute, which opened to a V, and hold a lit match to it, transfixed by the transference of flame as it leapt onto the surface of the material, dancing across it, and reduced it to grey, flimsy ashes. When everything was burnt up, he would pour water over the ashes and close the chute. His father never caught on to what he was doing, and Tien Chen was careful to cover his tracks.

His love of starting fires grew over time, though he never allowed it to get out of hand. Tien Chen knew the limits of what he was doing, and was wary of drawing undue attention to himself. It was something deeply personal, and he could not see how anyone else would understand. Tien Chen burnt all his primary school textbooks after he completed his PSLE; he told his father he had donated the books in a charity drive conducted in school for underprivileged students. His father had not suspected anything.

Likewise, right after he took his O-Levels—and not knowing how he had fared for his examinations—he tossed his books and study materials into the fire. He brought them down to the grass field beside his block, where there were large soot-darkened cylindrical burners for burning joss paper. Standing as close as he could to the pyre, the heat an unbearably intimate thing, he watched as the pages of his History textbook curled into tight rolls as the flames swept across the words and photographs—rubber trade in Malaysia, the Japanese Occupation, the state of emergency in Singapore in 1948—reducing them to heaving black feathers. He fed the books to the fire one by one. Back home, with his skin still tingling from its proximity to the fire, he noticed the hair on his knuckles and forearms were burnt into screwy twists, the tips gelled into pin-headed nobs. The smell of his singed hair was something he could never quite describe—charred, faintly synthetic, like burnt plastic—though he found it oddly familiar, personal.

The only things he did not burn were the books his father had bought for him, though he had tried once when he was nine and had only just discovered his fascination with fires. He had picked out a tattered book on dinosaurs in the Cretaceous period, the dog-eared pages already coming loose from the spine. He had barely brought the matchstick to the cover of the book when he felt a strange, sharp twist in his guts, and had to put out the budding flame with his bare hand. The act of saving the book left a red mark on his palm, which faded after a few days. There were other things he could burn, tons of things that were worthless, useless, even pointless.

As an adult, whenever Tien Chen tried to remember how and when he had first started burning himself, he would recall this childhood attempt to burn the dinosaurs book: the initial rush of excitement, followed almost instantly by an equal and confounding mix of guilt and relief. The pain—a sizzling tingle that crawled under his skin—had an immediate, sobering effect on him, sharpening his senses so acutely that he no longer felt temporal. His whole existence was reduced to the small patch of reddened skin the fire had licked. Even though the pain was intense, Tien Chen was undaunted by it. And the relief, when it came, was unlike anything he had felt before—as if he were tearing through a thick, sticky membrane and leaping into sudden light, the air flooding his lungs.

Two weeks after the first incident, he tried it again, bringing a lit match to his left thumb; the flame teased his skin with several flickers before it bit firmly into his flesh. He gasped, but held on till the match burnt itself out. The pain blinded him momentarily, until he took a long breath and felt the surge of relief inundating him. A blister formed where the flame had touched him, and in the days that followed, he would finger it tenderly, nudging the sac of pus under his skin, trying to rekindle the memory of the fire-sting in his head. He did not find this strange, or apportion any meaning to it. The act and his response to it were merely physical, he reasoned, and he only wanted to relive the sensation again and again. It was a private matter, a small part of his life that he could hold on to. He could not quite understand the significance of his actions, though he felt intensely—almost obsessively—for them.

Naturally, he kept this from his father, who had not suspected anything. Tien Chen was careful not to make his wounds too visible. He always allowed an existing burn to heal first, to develop a scab, before he burnt himself again. He restricted himself to certain parts of his body that were either common areas for injuries—palms, elbows, knees, heels—or completely hidden, like the inner thigh and pelvis. At first, he used matchsticks; later, in secondary school, he started using lighters. With the former, Tien Chen could always endure till the matchstick burnt out, but with the latter, he had to break away when the pain became too agonising, holding out till the very last moment before he was overwhelmed.

From all this, he learnt to exercise and exert self-control, and to discern when the desire to burn himself was just a whim, and when it was something he desperately needed to clear the chaos of thoughts in his head. When he held a flame to his skin, his mind dissolved, and all that existed was a gulf he could easily slip into. While he still enjoyed burning things and possessions that were worthless to him, deep inside he was aware that they were two entirely separate fixations, each bearing its own merits and inexplicable pleasures, and he took great care not to confuse one with the other.

Because of the nature of his father's work, Tien Chen was alone at home most of the time. Besides reading, Tien Chen devoted a good part of his time to cleaning the flat and putting away anything he could burn in a corner of the storeroom. The pile of unwanted stuff never grew beyond the weekly hoard of Chinese newspapers, flyers and unopened letters. He liked things to be in place, arranged in a certain way, kept under covers or in storage. As a result, the flat stayed utterly clutter-free. His father never said a word about his efforts, but Tien Chen could sense his approval in the approbative gaze sweeping across the almost bare living room. Tien Chen took a fair amount of pride in the knowledge that he was doing something that helped to keep their lives in order—neat, tidy, manageable.

Up till the time he joined the workforce after serving his national service, Tien Chen led a solitary life with very few demands. He tried dating a fellow classmate once, in his first year of polytechnic: a short, stout girl who was chatty and outgoing, but the whole thing petered out after two months. The girl left him, citing a clash of personalities—"*you're just too quiet and aloof*"—and he had remained apprehensive about getting into another relationship after that. He could not grasp the benefits of being in a relationship—the endless talking, the amount of time spent in another's presence, the meals and walks and movies. During the months of dating his classmate, Tien Chen had felt a constant sense of restlessness and anxiety, uncertain whether he was doing the right thing or saying what needed to be said at the right time. The gaps between her words were the hardest to fathom. He never knew what she truly meant: did she want something, was she happy or unhappy, was it a yes or no or maybe. The only time he felt a sense of relief was at the end of each date when he finally dropped her off at her doorstep. Of course, he had not minded the touching and kissing, but it came with a cost he was not sure he could keep up for long. So Tien Chen was neither surprised nor upset when the girl initiated a break-up; it had felt as if he were finally freed to pick up his life once again, to have all his senses returned to him.

He still dated once in a while, in the final year of polytechnic and in the army, but he never allowed these dates to develop into a serious relationship. Early on, his father had asked once or twice about his life outside of work, and each time Tien Chen had told him plainly that he wasn't seeing anyone. His father never pressed further, only saying that these things took time, and that there wasn't a hurry to find someone if he wasn't ready. And since Tien Chen was relatively happy with the way he was living his life then and rarely felt the need to complicate it, he remained single through his early twenties. *Hell is other people,* he reminded himself, *why bother?*

For a while, Tien Chen believed what he had told himself about what he needed or didn't need from other people. Then one day he set his eyes on a young woman, a zi-char stall helper who had just started working in the same kopitiam as his father. Tien Chen first noticed her when she approached him with a laminated menu. As she was highlighting the specials, Tien Chen could not help but study the deep dimples punctuating the sides of her mouth. She spoke Mandarin with a Malaysian accent. After ordering a plate of beef hor fun, he asked her where she was from. Ipoh. He wanted to ask a few more things, but she had already turned away, walking back to place the order with the chef.

He took his time with the plate of beef hor fun, and watched the woman as she went around the kopitiam, taking food orders and serving the dishes. Something pressed hard against his heart, a terribly new and foreign feeling. For the rest of the week, Tien Chen had his dinners at the kopitiam after work and ordered food from the young woman. He would stay until his father knocked off from work, and together they would walk back home. *You're not sick of the food at the kopitiam ah,* his father said, *always eating the same thing.* Tien Chen shook his head and said nothing. What could he tell his father when he was still trying to figure out why he was so irrationally and compulsively drawn to the young zi-char stall helper?

During every meal at the kopitiam, Tien Chen took great pains to appear casual when he asked the young woman simple questions, so as to mask his interest in her. Forthcoming and artless, she gave brief, tidy replies that always ended with a slight smile. He liked the sound of her voice; it reminded him of a breeze caught between the shadows of leaves: soft, supple, lulling. He found himself greatly stirred by it, having heard nothing like it before, something so otherworldly, so mysterious. It sounded silly when he thought about it, but how else was he to explain the profound effect it had on him? At night, lying in bed, he would conjure up her voice and imagine what it would take to possess it. He wanted to hold it—this object of infinite, unspeakable beauty—close to him, for he felt like he was the only one who could behold its true worth, who could hear it for what it was.

No, this is too silly, he reasoned, *too goddamn silly.*

"So what do you want to eat today?" she would say as she stood by the table with a writing pad in hand, waiting for him to decide. Each time, Tien Chen hesitated before uttering the name of the first dish that popped into his head. When the woman left with his food order, Tien Chen would pick up the Chinese newspapers he had bought at a newsstand at the bus interchange and pretend to scan the headlines. But his eyes were constantly on the woman, tracking her movements and noting her gestures, trying to sift her voice out of the cacophony in the kopitiam.

By the end of the third week, Tien Chen drummed up the courage to ask her out as he was paying for his meal. The young woman smiled as she considered his suggestion briefly, and agreed. He arranged for a meal on her day off—*lunch would be better for me, if it's okay with you,* she said—and offered to pick her up from her place. She declined the pick-up—*too inconvenient*—and proposed to meet him directly at the venue.

They slowly warmed up to each other over lunch, proceeding from topics about work and leisure into discussions about family and personal interests. From the conversation, Tien Chen learnt about her family background (*too big, too many mouths to feed, my parents really had a hard time taking care of us*) and found out why she had to come to Singapore to work (*the money is good, and I really want to broaden my world, to see other things, other people*). At the mention of other people, Tien Chen suddenly turned morose, though he masked it with a long sip of water; he did not dare to probe further on this, and since Yifan—he chanted the name privately, engraving the crisp, honeyed syllables into the grooves of his mind—had already moved on from the topic, he could not possibly bring it up again without rousing her suspicion.

Yifan was 24, four years younger than Tien Chen but by all appearances, she looked hardly a day older than 18. *What's your secret*, Tien Chen asked teasingly, and Yifan broke into a spell of giggles, shaking her head. By the time they finished their meal—they had ordered two rounds of dessert—they were talking and laughing freely, like close friends.

I really like your voice, said Tien Chen, as they walked to the train station where they parted.

What do you like about it? she asked. *Are you making fun of how I speak?* With that, she let out another laugh.

After that, Tien Chen had his meals at the kopitiam whenever he could, even on weekends. He would spend hours there, nursing several glasses of coffee, waiting for any opportunity to talk to Yifan. A week after their first date he had asked Yifan out again and brought her to a highly-regarded restaurant. She had chided him lightly for being too extravagant for her tastes, and said she much preferred low-key places with affordable prices. He went along with her suggestions: to him, the meals were only a pretext to see her and spend time with her. He liked how she was slowly becoming comfortable with him, evident from the easy banter that went on without a break. There was never a dull moment in their conversations: everything seemed lighter and brighter in her presence. He lapped up her words, as if they were a special source of nutrient that fed something famished and empty inside him. He had never felt the same way with the other girls he had dated, this desire for intimacy that pushed him towards the edge of a greater unknown, this burgeoning sense of love that was all teeth and hunger.

At the end of their second month of courtship, Tien Chen finally asked Yifan whether she was seeing anyone else. *Why?* she asked.

I'm curious, that's all, Tien Chen said. *And also I want to know whether I've any competition.*

Yifan laughed, and put a hand on Tien Chen's. Her eyes shone with a mirthful yet impenetrable gleam, and she said nothing. With the question out in the open, a burden finally lifted from Tien Chen's chest, to be instantaneously replaced by a new unexpected one. *Would you be my—*

Before he could finish his request, Yifan started laughing again, breaking his confidence. *Let me think about it,* she said.

For days, Tien Chen moved like a man suspended in a trance, unable to get a bearing on the life around him. In order to feel something tangible, he burnt himself twice, thrice a day, on his palms and inner thighs. *The pain is real,* he reasoned, *you feel it, it's there.* Looking around his room after each session, as the pain melted into the dark recesses of his body, Tien Chen acutely felt the limits of his life; how threadbare it seemed. He had steeped his whole life in loneliness—how little he had cared for anything or anyone until now. The feeling was a terrifying crush against his heart that he couldn't do anything about.

One night, he approached Yifan after she knocked off from work and made his confession of love. She listened quietly as he forced the words out of his mouth, stammering and tripping over them. He felt his face contorting into strange expressions to convey what he was saying, and he saw how Yifan's face, too, went through a different sort of transition, from disbelief to understanding. Her eyes were a shade darker than usual. When he finally came to the end of his confession, there was a heavy pause, and then Yifan leant into him. Tien Chen took her into his embrace, hanging onto her like a lifeline.

• • •

In the early stages of their courtship, Tien Chen was extremely attentive to Yifan's needs. He left messages on her phone in the morning, and called her every afternoon during his lunch break to check on her. Their phone chats were filled with trivial and mundane matters that were rendered fresh and unique to Tien Chen. Every aspect of Yifan was new and thrillingly special; every question he asked provoked a steady stream of enthusiastic answers that opened up to more questions from him. Where does the mystery of a person begin, Tien Chen thought to himself more than once, and will it ever cease? The more he knew about Yifan, the more he realised how little he knew her, as if every door of knowledge he opened led into a new corridor of closed doors, stretching into an infinite distance. Yet this awareness did not daunt him in any way. He loved her, and wanted to be with her. He would take his time to know her; he would pare the layers till he reached her core. When he'd made that decision, Tien Chen was able to quell his fear and settle into the relationship.

Tien Chen invited Yifan back to his place on a Tuesday, her day off. When she entered the flat, she expressed surprise at its bareness and cleanliness. She padded around daintily in her socks, as if she were afraid of leaving any marks or stains.

Don't worry, you don't have to be so self-conscious lah, Tien Chen said.

Can't tell you're such a neat freak, she said.

When they finished their dinner of chicken burgers, fries and milk shakes, Tien Chen cleared away the wrappers and emptied packs of chilli sauce. Coming out of the kitchen, he saw Yifan standing beside the altar, looking at the framed portrait of his mother. Yifan smiled at him when she sensed his presence, softening her expression. The portrait was an old photograph, a studio shot, and in it, Tien Chen's mother was glancing away at an angle, her gaze shy and cryptic. He had seen this photograph all his life, and there was nothing in it that he had not filed away in his mind: puffy bangs, thick dark lips, and the gentle resoluteness in his mother's eyes. Tien Chen knew he had inherited some of his mother's features, something his father alluded to when he was younger. When he was 13, he had taken the portrait down from the altar and set it in front of a mirror, searching for some kind of resemblance in the reflected images. He studied every detail of his mother's face, as if willing for something to click into place, to make some sense.

You've got her eyes, Yifan said. Tien Chen quickly glanced at the photo; he could not see any similarity whatsoever, then or now.

When they were seated on the sofa, Yifan said, *I lost my father several years ago. Lung cancer. My mother was devastated, I think, but she didn't say anything to any of us.*

As Tien Chen listened to Yifan's story, his mind went down a tunnel of buried memories. Long-dormant images awakened: his mother, his father, the years of their relationship, the march of time—death connects everyone, the one unshakeable certainty. He knew almost nothing about his mother, and next to nothing about his father, though he was still alive, and they had stayed in the same flat for over thirty years. Yet now, listening to Yifan—her voice, the words coming from her mouth, braided with meaning and hidden significance—he felt a sudden sense of loss for something that had eluded him over the years. Who was his father? Who was he to him? Tien Chen was grateful for the fact that his father had fed him, taken care of him, and provided for him, and that they had made up their lives as they went along. But was it enough? Tien Chen wasn't sure now. He knew he had allowed things to slip, to fall into the cracks, and the awareness of that loss struck him anew.

He did not know how lost he was in his own thoughts, but when he felt a pressure on his arm, he blinked and stared once again into Yifan's eyes.

Where did you go? she asked.

I'm here, he said, *I'm listening.*

The first four months of the relationship were as smooth-sailing as Tien Chen had hoped. Though they had different work schedules—Tien Chen worked a nine-to-six job as a junior draughtsman in an architecture firm, while Yifan knocked off around ten-thirty at night—they managed to meet at least five times a week. Tien Chen had his dinner every weekday night at the kopitiam without fail. By that time, his father was aware of their relationship, although he kept out of their hair and did not pry. As far as Tien Chen could tell, his father had already liked Yifan even before they were a couple. Yifan, on her part, reinforced the good impression she had made by seeking Tien Chen's father out for conversations during lulls at the kopitiam, and giving him a hand in clearing empty glasses and beer bottles from the tables whenever she could.

Though Tien Chen would have liked to spend all his time with Yifan, the latter was adamant on having some time alone, for 'personal space'.

Why? Tien Chen asked.

So you won't get sick of me lah, seeing me all the time, she replied.

For one thing, she never allowed him to send her home after work every night. *There's no need,* she told him, *it'll be very late by the time you get home, so save yourself the trouble since you have to work early the next day.* Seeing the logic in her explanation, Tien Chen never offered again.

Still, he would send her a text every night to check on her whereabouts after work, and would wait till she replied before he slept. Some nights there would be no reply, and he would get so worried that he would start calling her repeatedly. The first few times she did not reply or pick up the calls, Tien Chen got into such a fix that he could not stay still or sleep the whole night. When he brought it up later, Yifan was quick to appease him by claiming that her mobile phone was on silent mode, or that she had fallen asleep right after she came home.

After these early episodes, Yifan became more prompt in her replies, though they never went beyond anything perfunctory: *I'm home, I'm fine, okay, good night.* Some nights, her replies would come two or three hours later, and Tien Chen would wonder where she was or what she was doing during those hours. It was unimaginable to him that Yifan would have anything else to do after work; he knew she had few interests apart from watching TVB and Korean dramas and playing Candy Crush on her phone. She had little patience for shopping or sports, and given half a chance, would prefer to spend her free time at home, catching up on sleep in the three-room flat she shared with five other Malaysians who worked office jobs.

Tien Chen had his concerns. But when he tried to stay as late as he could at the kopitiam, she would nudge him to go home, telling him not to wait for her to knock off. When he refused, Yifan became more insistent, a look of annoyance flitting across her features, and he had to back off immediately. Knowing his tendency to overthink, Tien Chen chose to play down his overt curiosity and assure himself that there was really nothing to worry about, that he trusted her.

Yet even at the peak of his happiness with Yifan, Tien

Chen still kept up his habit of burning himself. While the frequency dwindled during the intense early months of courtship, it was still something he gave himself to almost unthinkingly. To keep Yifan from finding out about his habit, Tien Chen took extra precautions. He restricted himself to areas that could easily be covered up—the inner thighs and pelvis, the heels and soles. No more burning on his arms or palms. And he was diligent in making sure the wounds were properly attended to with gels and plasters and dressings; he did not want them to fester and worsen. It had happened once in polytechnic, while he had been preparing for his final-year exams. He was burning himself three, four times a day then; the urgency was unstoppable, almost physical in its appetite, and he yielded to it all the time. He had neglected the treatment of his wounds and they had suppurated, oozing thick, putrid pus. It had taken almost three weeks for the wounds to heal, during which he had to avoid his father's glances, locking himself up in his room and pleading the need to mug for the exams. After that incident Tien Chen learnt to rotate the spots on his body where he burnt himself, and allow existing injuries to heal.

Some of the wounds had hardened into a series of discoloured scars and keloids, which Tien Chen tried to lighten with anti-scarring creams. He reminded himself not to appear too self-conscious when he first held Yifan's hand after their fourth date. Later, when she asked about the star-shaped scars on his palms, he had lied, claiming that they were from injuries he had got from his army days as a weapons specialist in the infantry.

You know lah, trying to be garang, to impress my men, he said.

You have plenty of scars, she said, *your arms and legs too, you must have a very tough army life.* To which Tien Chen responded with a nonplussed shrug. He had not expected Yifan to pay enough attention to his body to notice the scars. After that incident he made a great deal of effort to dress more appropriately when he met her, keeping to long-sleeved shirts and pants or jeans. Though he worried sometimes whether or not Yifan would ever find out about his habit, he knew there was nothing to stop him from doing it till then. And if his secret ever came to light, Tien Chen wondered whether he would have the wherewithal to put a stop to the habit that had sustained and comforted him for so many years.

The first time Tien Chen decided to trail Yifan was a Friday, after she had texted him to cancel their after-work supper. She was tired and wanted to rest early, she said.

From a hidden corner of the void deck in a nearby block Tien Chen watched her leave the kopitiam, carrying a bag of food. She boarded a feeder bus, and Tien Chen quickly hailed a taxi to follow it. She alighted several stops later, beside a neighbourhood park on the edge of Ang Mo Kio. She did not notice Tien Chen watching her from across the street.

What was she doing here at this hour, Tien Chen wondered, his mind forging ahead for plausible reasons. She did not have any relatives or friends—at least none she had told him about—living in Singapore, in this estate. He watched as she straightened out her hair with a few brusque strokes and walked to the block beside the bus stop. By the time he reached the lift lobby, he had lost her, though he saw that the lift had stopped on the ninth floor. He took the lift up and, stepping out gingerly, looked down the dark stretch of corridor. Who was she visiting? Was she seeing someone else? Tien Chen's thoughts tore in different directions, and he broke out in cold sweat, his breaths becoming short and laboured.

He padded softly down the corridor, and stopped outside a flat when he saw her sandals. Through the frosted-glass windows, he saw the dim light from the living room. Standing very still, he strained to hear the sounds coming from within: low muffled voices, an occasional burst of laughter—Yifan's. A man's gruff voice; Tien Chen could barely catch what the man was saying. Who was he? Who was he to Yifan? A hard lump grew in his throat and he felt a narrow band tightening around his head, signalling the onset of a pounding headache. Tien Chen did not know how long he stood outside the flat that first time, but when he saw someone coming down the corridor in his direction, he fled the scene as if he had been caught trying to break in. He escaped down the stairwell, and walked the long way home, his mind held in an unbreakable spell. Back home, he took out the lighter and held the flame against an old, scabby wound on his inner thigh, burning his flesh to an inflamed, weeping ring.

He did not bring up this matter with Yifan when they met the next day for dinner and a movie. He observed Yifan from a great detached distance, analysing her every move, every word, in detail—what did she mean, what was she saying, why was she feeling or acting in a particular manner? In all ways, she was the same—genial, amenable, attentive—and yet in Tien Chen's eyes, she could not be more different, an apparition of a woman emerging from some unknown depth. She had chosen to keep parts of her life hidden from him, for reasons he could not fathom. Who was the man—an ex-lover, or a current one? Tien Chen felt pained at the thought that Yifan was seeing someone else, that she was two-timing him. He knew he had to speak up—why was he still keeping mum?—but something held him back. He needed to figure out the missing fragments of the puzzle. To come out directly with his fear would have been unimaginable; he knew he would put a vast strain on their still-young relationship if he were to confront her at this stage. He needed time to find out more.

And so he kept up the surveillance. Yifan rarely changed her nightly ritual—leaving the kopitiam at ten-thirty, a bag of food in her hand, then taking the bus to the flat where the man lived. Some nights, she stayed for an hour or so, often taking the last bus to the interchange where she would transfer to another feeder service that would take her home. On other nights, when she had a day off from work the next day, she lingered till the early hours—once, she had left the man's place at four am—before taking a taxi home. Never once did she spend a full night at his place, Tien Chen observed. As usual, every night, Yifan would send him a text to assure him that she was back home, and it pained Tien Chen to read these messages as he loitered along the corridor or at the void deck, waiting for Yifan to emerge from the flat. The wait each time felt endless, excruciating. After the fourth night, he brought along the lighter and took it out periodically to burn himself whenever he felt his mind slipping into a deepening, despairing state.

He was into his third week of spying when he almost blew his cover. He was sitting on a stone bench beside a children's playground facing the block when Yifan walked out of the lift landing, heading for a path that cut through the field. He had barely enough time to hide himself behind the wall of the concrete slide, his heart thumping madly in his chest. When he sensed the coast was clear, he came out of hiding. He wasn't sure why, but an instinct bit him then, and he looked up and saw a dark figure—a man?—leaning against the parapet, smoking. From where Tien Chen was standing, he knew the man could not see him. He slipped back into the shadows and watched the man; while there was no way to discern any of the man's features, Tien Chen did not look away, drawn in fully by his presence. He left only when the man stubbed out the cigarette and threw it over the parapet. Pall Mall. Tien Chen picked up the half-burnt butt and stuffed it into his jeans.

The Sunday of the week Tien Chen found out about the other man, he brought Yifan home and made love to her. They went slowly at first, then all at once they tipped into the lovemaking, each surprised by the other's passion. He felt a lightness in his head as he cupped Yifan's breasts together and took the hard, raisin-sized nipples into his mouth, nibbling them. The nipples strained against the rough teasing of his tongue, wet with his saliva. When he moved his fingers lightly across the warm folds of her vulva and rubbed the nub of her clitoris, Yifan cried out as if he had scorched her. For a moment, he imagined the edge of a flame brushing against her vagina, touching her, and this image alone caused him to tremble violently, uncontrollably. He wanted to taste every inch, every hidden, secret part of her: the salty undersides of her breasts, the nooks of her armpits, the slick of skin that slid into her tight ass-bud; he wanted her whole, in all her different states: sad, ecstatic, unbridled, lost, hungry. Putting his tongue into her thick fleshy folds, he coaxed and licked every drop of juice that flowed out of her, and holding the briny taste on his tongue, he was reminded of the sea, of the secret depth it held, and the invisible lives that came and went in the dark, sunless world. He was a part of that world, in and through Yifan, and for as long as he held onto her, that world was his. From somewhere far away, he thought he heard his name, a name that did not mean anything to him. It was Yifan calling out to him, calling him to her.

Tien Chen opened his eyes; the sight of Yifan filled his vision. He took a deep breath and kissed her. He had her; it was enough. When she came, she shuddered for a few unbroken seconds, before collapsing into him.

Yet even after that, and other sessions of lovemaking, Tien Chen did not feel he had Yifan completely. She still eluded him when she was with him, even when he was inside her. And the secrecy of his sleuthing did little to lessen the love he had for her; in fact, it did the opposite. It deepened the mystery of Yifan held in his mind, which compounded his own sense of bewilderment and longing. He had never wanted her more than in those weeks that he knew she was seeing the other man; he needed to possess her—to make a claim on her—even the parts that were inaccessible to him. He kissed her more fervently and gripped her hand at every chance, as if she would slip away if he did not hold on tightly to her. She gave in to him, at first in bemused surprise, and later, with greater abandonment.

Sometimes, when they were kissing, Tien Chen would imagine the man's tongue in Yifan's mouth, teasing, searching, wet and slippery with intention and desire. He imagined his hands—the other man's—on Yifan, as he held them behind her back, down her butt, on the firm curves of her breasts, on her thighs. Was this how the man would hold her, how he would trail his fingers across her body or taste her skin? He was racked with doubt and jealousy, and at the same time he could not deny the effect the thoughts of Yifan and the man had on him, opening up a pit inside him that allowed his darker yearnings to come unbound. In his imagination and actions he was a different man—or was he the other man?

He wondered whether Yifan knew exactly who she was with when they were together, whether she really, truly wanted this other man he was inhabiting—alive in another skin—or someone else entirely. Does love always divide the lover, splitting him into numerous other beings? Did Yifan come to him as an amalgam of different parts, of different identities? Which one of her did he love then—the woman in front of him, or the one in his imagination, conjured up with words and wild fancy? He did not know.

Some nights, when Yifan slept over at his place, her mobile phone would buzz intermittently with messages. She smiled when she read the messages, though she never revealed what they were about, or from whom. Sometimes, when she was in the toilet or kitchen, Tien Chen would pick up her phone and read the new messages: *Wrote a new story, want to read it to you. Come over soon? I miss you. Any plans tonight?* Because Yifan always deleted the messages she read—no old messages in the inbox, only the latest ones—there was no way Tien Chen could form a clear story in his head about the relationship between her and the other man.

If Yifan knew about his snooping, she did not let on. On her part, she managed to keep up appearances, not minding when Tien Chen refused to do anything on her day off apart from a long session of lovemaking at his place and staying in afterward. *I can cook for you,* he said, *you have everything you need here.*

But aren't you bored? she said.

No, not with you. And if there was a choice, he would have thrown away her mobile phone, so she would not be so distracted with any new messages.

When Yifan needed to head back home, Tien Chen would accompany her right to her doorstep. She lived in the western part of Ang Mo Kio, and usually they took the twenty-minute walk back. By this time her flat mates were well acquainted with Tien Chen, and made small talk with him when they saw him. Yifan shared a small, tidy bedroom with another Malaysian, a girl from Taiping, who worked shifts in an electronics-manufacturing factory, and whom Tien Chen had just met twice. The bedroom held only the barest of furniture: a peeling cupboard, two beds with thin mattresses, an aluminium hanging rack, and a tiny bedside table. Four other occupants, all women, took up the other bedrooms, and there was never a dull or quiet moment in the flat. A heavy miasma of smells hung in the air: spicy ramen, citrus shampoo, floor cleanser. The TV was always on, no matter what time of the day it was or whether anyone was watching: a drone of white noise against the fuzzy background of chatter and voices. Once, Tien Chen had asked Yifan to move in with him, but she declined. *I've got used to this,* she said, *and all of us get along fine anyway.*

In some ways, Yifan was very much like Tien Chen: her side of the room was kept extremely clean and sparse, with beige-coloured bedclothes; all her belongings were kept out of sight in the cupboard or in the small suitcase under the bed. The smell of talcum powder lingered lightly in the room, one Tien Chen associated closely with Yifan.

The first time he spent a night in her room—he persisted, knowing that her roommate had gone back to Taiping for a family visit over a long weekend—they made love quietly on her bed. *Don't make too much noise, the walls are thin, they can hear us,* she said.

Let them hear, I'm not ashamed, he said.

But I live here, and it's embarrassing for me. She covered

Tien Chen's mouth with her hand when he was about to come, and they had laughed at the end of it.

Because of his pressing and unspoken curiosity about how she lived, Tien Chen began to devise ways to spend his nights over at her place. More than anything, the time he spent at Yifan's gave him the opportunity to find out whatever he could about her from the things she kept and the possessions she had. He peeked into the cupboard and suitcase whenever she was in the shower and went through her clothes and books, hoping to uncover some letters or a diary, but she kept none of these things. There was an old Samsung phone hidden behind a clump of underwear, but it was dead. In one of the pouches, he discovered an old photo of Yifan and a few classmates in uniform. She had straight shoulder-length hair then, held back with a hairclip, and was leaning against a tall, lanky boy with a narrow, pimply face. Tien Chen studied the boy's face; there was nothing distinct or prominent in his features. He took it out a few more times after the initial discovery, trying to commit the boy's face to memory, but it never stuck. To ask Yifan about him would betray his snooping, so he kept the questions to himself.

Tien Chen also looked into a black accordion file where she kept her travel and work permit documents, and took down the address of her hometown in Ipoh. Among the papers, he found several pieces of printouts. Fragments of stories. One was about a band of ancient swordsmen exacting revenge on a rival group, another about a boy's fascination with collecting dead moths. There was one he was particularly interested in, a story about a fox spirit. He read it several times, and because the fragments were disjointed, he was only able to form a rough outline in his head of what the story was about. Who wrote these stories—Yifan? If not, where did she get these stories? Who gave them to her? And why was she keeping them? Tien Chen hid the fox story in his bag and brought it home. He had expected, even secretly hoped, that Yifan would bring up the missing story somehow—was it important to her at all?—but she never once showed any signs of noticing its absence.

His obsession grew as time passed. He started to steal other things whenever he went over to Yifan's place: a comb, a stick of lipstick, an old T-shirt, a pair of panties that had lost its elasticity. He would stash the items in a small messenger bag and put it in a disused army haversack which he hid at the back of his wardrobe. He would take Yifan's things out on nights she was not able to meet him, running the comb through his hair or applying a gloss of lipstick on his lips and kissing the reflection in the mirror. He would slip into Yifan's underwear and, lying on his bed, imagined running his tongue over her hardened nipples and the wet flaps of her vulva. Working his hand frantically inside the underwear, he would ejaculate furiously, the thick gluey semen rising through the lacy fabric. After he was through with his ritual, he would take up the lighter and work the flame across his skin, the edge of pain bringing his mind to heel. He would skip out of existence for a brief moment and become absolutely nothing, only a bright, dying pinpoint of illumination, now here, now gone. He often felt calmer after each burning, his senses returned, focused.

Because he was burning himself every day, Tien Chen became careless about monitoring his wounds. He still ensured that they were treated immediately after each burning by applying lotions and aloe vera gel, and hiding them with plasters and dressings, but there were simply too many for him to keep track of constantly. Some of the wounds started to leak, while others grew itchy with scabs. On busy days at work, he sometimes did not realise the blood and pus had seeped through his work shirt until he noticed the stains on the papers and files on his desk. He began keeping a supply of dressings in his drawer at work, along with a backup of dark-coloured work shirts. He got so worried that he started to skip lunch with his colleagues, choosing to eat in at the office pantry.

One night, whilst he was lying in bed with Yifan, she turned to him, a strange, perplexed expression on her face. *I know what you have been doing,* she said.

Tien Chen's heart took a few lurching leaps; his skin went cold. *Why are you hiding this from me?* she asked. *You know that I know, right?* Tien Chen kept mum. *You can tell me.*

Still, he maintained his silence. *This, all these, I know what they are,* she said, holding up his hand, *these scars. You did this to yourself, right?*

Though they were lying side by side, Tien Chen had never felt more distant from Yifan, as if they existed in two separate, vastly different dimensions. After some time, Tien Chen nodded.

Why can't you be frank with me? Why can't you tell me this? she said.

For the same reason you can't, or won't, tell me about your relationship with the other man, Tien Chen had wanted to say, but knew it wasn't the right time to bring it up. *It's nothing, you don't have to worry, just a bad habit.*

Her gaze drilled into him, a fleeting hint of sympathy—pity?—in her stare. She took a deep breath. *I used to cut myself when I was sixteen. Small cuts at first, very superficial, like light scratches on my skin. They didn't hurt too much.*

And then I began to cut more, and deeper too. I'm not sure why I did it then. For release, for attention, I don't know. I wasn't depressed or anything, or at least I didn't think I was. I told myself it was nothing serious. Some of my classmates were cutting themselves as well, I saw the lines on their wrists and hands. I thought it was a passing phase, something a stupid teenager would do, like smoking or shoplifting. And I did it for a long time, through my adolescence, and then I didn't want to do it anymore. I decided one day to stop and forced myself to follow through with my decision.

What made you stop? Tien Chen asked.

Something happened, which made me realise... Her words trailed off.

What was it, Tien Chen pressed.

Yifan shrugged, and turned the topic back to Tien Chen. *I know it's hard to quit this if you've been doing it for a long time. I'm not going to pester you to give it up. I know you have your limits. But you need to decide whether it'll do you any good in the long run. You have to make that decision, not me,* she said. Then, holding Tien Chen's hand towards her, she touched the still-tender wound in the middle of his palm.

For a long time after that night, Tien Chen took great effort not to burn himself whenever he felt the urge rising inside him. He knew its shape and pulse intimately, and to overcome it he took to burning other things in the flat, starting with his own. The clothes were the first to go: his old army uniforms and PT attire, work shirts and pants showing signs of wear and tear, T-shirts and bermudas that had not been worn for some time, loose-necked socks. He cleared them in small batches, burning the clothes in the soot-covered bin beside the refuse compound in the neighbourhood. He applied only one rule to the frenzy of clearing his stuff: keep only the essentials. By the end of the second week, his wardrobe was down to just five work shirts, two pairs of black pants, one pair of dress shoes, one pair of running shoes, one tie, three pairs of socks, five pairs of underwear, seven T-shirts, two bermudas, one belt. He stared into the bare cupboard, and the empty spaces inside filled him with an irrational sense of achievement.

Next: the stacks of CDs and DVDs. He ripped their contents onto his hard disk, keeping nothing. When it seemed he had burnt all that he could of his belongings, Tien Chen finally turned to the books his father had bought for him when he was a child. There was a bookshelf in his room where he kept them in neat, straight rows, and he took pride in still having these keen reminders of his childhood around. *Jungles of the World*: a present for his seventh birthday; *Lost Ancient Civilisations*: for coming in fifth in class when he was in Primary Five; *UFOs and Other Supernatural Phenomena*: for scoring high marks on a science test. He had once held these books as faithful companions, providing paths into all kinds of knowledge about the world while keeping at bay the sharp loneliness he had always felt as a child, left alone in the flat when his father was at work.

But Tien Chen could no longer connect these books with his childhood, and whatever effect they had on him was long gone. To him, they were just tattered edges and age-faded pages, dusty and useless. He had thought about giving them to the Salvation Army or the karung guni man who came to his block once a fortnight, but the idea that they would fall into the hands of some stranger did not appeal to him, and so he pushed back the decision every time. This time, he refused to be deterred. He filled up a storage box with as many books as it could hold and carried them to the burner-bin.

He picked up the first book, *Dinosaurs and Other Prehistoric Reptiles*, and brought the lighter to a page and watched as the tiny flicker of flame trembled and moved across the glossy surface, blackening the words and pictures. He threw the book into the bin and waited for the fire to catch on. As he burnt the books, he stood close to the bin and felt the waves of heat licking him, tingling under his skin.

It took him three days to burn everything, in the end. Later, he dismantled the bookshelf and burnt it as well. His father had come in with an armful of folded laundry one night and surveyed Tien Chen's bedroom. *What happened to the books?* he said.

I gave them away, Tien Chen replied, not looking at him. His father shook his head and left the room.

The amount of stuff in his bedroom dwindled. Some nights when he coughed, he could hear an echo bouncing off the walls. At the same time, over the weeks, the items he took from Yifan and hoarded in his old army bag multiplied. He took only what he assumed Yifan would never miss: a scrunchie, a pen, an old photograph of her (from a stack she kept in her suitcase), an unused tube of face cream. He bought a bigger storage bag, and also a lock. Whenever he stayed over at Yifan's, he would scan her belongings minutely, assessing the next item to take, weighing the risk. On nights he left empty-handed, Tien Chen would feel dispossessed, as if he had been unfairly deprived of some vital material need. He could not understand why: this need that demanded so much to be sated. He had Yifan—he possessed her in all imaginable ways, he thought—but still something was lacking, something invisible but substantial. He took and took, as if he were trying to gather and assemble all the pieces of her, and yet there were always some more missing pieces he could not quite find. He did not want to give up, though it felt like there was a long way to go still.

One night, on a weekday, Yifan saw him standing at the block of flats opposite the kopitiam. Tien Chen had not moved fast enough to hide behind a pillar, and so he waited while Yifan walked up to him, her face strangely calm, inscrutable.

What are you doing here? she said.

Nothing, I was feeling restless at home, he said, glancing at the bag of food in her hand.

He waited for her explanation, but the answer never came. Instead, Yifan stared into his face, reading something there that he was not able to conceal. He felt exposed.

How long have you been doing this? she said.

What, he feigned, *what are you talking about?*

The look on her face shifted. Barely suppressing an undertone of chill and impatience, she asked: *Have you been following me?*

Tien Chen stayed silent, his insides balling up into a tight fist.

I can't talk to you now, I don't think I can say anything, she said.

Tien Chen reached out for her, and Yifan reflexively blocked the gesture with her raised hand, letting go of the bag of food. It fell to her feet with a wet thud, spilling everything across her sandals.

Why are you doing this? Tien Chen asked, taking another step towards her.

I don't know how to explain it to you now. With that, Yifan turned on her heel and moved away from Tien Chen, her back hunched but resolute.

Yifan, he called out. She did not turn around.

That night, Tien Chen called and sent her messages, and only received dead silence as reply.

For a week, he did not hear from Yifan. He turned up at the kopitiam for dinner but Yifan refused to acknowledge him, giving him a wide berth. He pleaded for a reply of sorts, through his messages. *I'm sorry. I just needed to know. Who is he? Who is he to you?* He heard nothing from her, and it almost drove him out of his mind. He took out Yifan's possessions from the bag and held them every night, trying to breathe some meaning into each piece of item. He took out the story of the fox spirit he had stolen from her, and read it repeatedly.

FOX FIRE GIRL

In his vivid, fretful dreams, Yifan was the fox spirit, making her way through a dark forest, running away (or towards?) some form of danger, her glistening sheen of fur catching the moonlight, slipping in and out of the shadows. He followed her (who was he in the dream, this moving presence? Another fox? A ghost?) for a while, coming so close he could smell the heavy dank scent of her sweaty fur, and hear the panting of her breath. She stopped from time to time, pricking up her ears to pick up the nocturnal noises, or sniffing the damp foggy air for signs of life. Did she sense his presence? Did she know he was there, beside her?

Every time, an anguished cry would sound out from somewhere in the dark, shattering the cloak of silence in the forest, breaking the grip of his dream. Tien Chen woke shivering to these visions in his dream, his limbs aching as if he had been traversing great distances.

At the end of the week, he could bear it no more; he took out the lighter and held it over his palm, the old scab softening in the heat of the flame. The pain swept over him, blinding, rapturous. He held himself still for as long as he could before he finally passed out, weeping pus and blood from the melted flesh.

Tien Chen woke up with a start, feeling someone nudge his arm. How long had he slept? His body felt weakened, pulverised, his head all light and spikes. A hand was put to his forehead—his father's hand. He tried to raise his body upright, but invisible weights pinned him down. A piss-yellow trickle of pus-blood dripped from his half-clenched palm onto the bedspread; he closed it. Short pulses of pain, claw-sharp.

He saw the shadow of his father moving out of the room and, a moment later, coming in with a damp towel. He pressed it gently against Tien Chen's palm, sending a shock of pain across his hand, up his arm. *You're having a fever,* he heard his father saying, *you're burning up.* In his mind's eye, Tien Chen saw the spread of red across the dead spaces inside him, creeping up the walls, filling up the air. He sensed a flurry of movements out of the corner of his eye, a glimpse of—paws? Pointy ears? Was it the fox? He breathed hard, choking on the gulps of air burning down his dry throat.

Here, take this, drink up, a voice whispered. He opened his mouth, a bitterness dissolving on his tongue. *Now lie back, sleep.* He resisted, but the effort sapped him completely. *Sleep now.*

He felt a tug on his other hand, and something slipped out of his grip, soft and smooth like a ribbon. He opened his eyes; the image of his father shimmered in the vision, holding a piece of—

Tien Chen suddenly groped the air and the sodden bedsheet around him. Yifan's T-shirt, her belongings, everything was gone. A dark thought sliced into his head: had he burnt them too?

He attempted to sit upright; a pair of hands pushed him back down. *I need to*—he spat out.

I have them, go to sleep. Rest now. A flutter of tremors echoed through his body, the flight of blind ravens. Tien Chen closed his eyes; darkness clamoured around him, beating weak, frantic wings. He could not sleep, he had to be awake, it was not over. The crunch of footsteps in the forest, the glint of a beast's eye, the hot, dying breaths—he slipped back into his fevered dream, trailing long shadows.

The next time he woke, everything was brighter, clearer. His head seemed wiped out, a blank slate. His right palm was swathed in gauze, a penumbra of blood peeking through the surface. Tien Chen glanced at his father's face, and looked away. Something in his father's expression hounded him for an answer, an explanation. *I don't understand why you've done this,* his father said, his brow creased. *Why?*

A sudden rage opened up inside Tien Chen, baring its teeth. *I'm sorry,* he said, finally, *it's nothing.*

For how long? A pained look claimed his father's features.

Don't ask, Tien Chen said. *I don't know, it doesn't matter, just forget it.*

His father continued to press for answers, but Tien Chen had fallen into an unbridgeable sullenness, pulling away. *I don't know what you want me to say, there's nothing to say. Just leave me alone, please, just forget everything.*

His father shook his head—in disgust? shame?—and left the room. In his absence, Tien Chen felt only the sting of his own anger, and a regret that had gouged a deep hole inside him.

The same afternoon, Yifan appeared in his room. He heard a knock on the bedroom door, and there she was, in a white chiffon blouse and capris, her face scrubbed of any expression or emotion. For a moment, she stood near his bed, undecided. Then she lowered herself and sat next to him. *Your father told me about you*, she said. *I just want to make sure you're okay.*

Tien Chen reached for her hand in her lap; she let him. *I miss you*, he said.

Yifan smiled, averting her gaze. Then she said: *He's a friend, a close friend. He's not well, and he needs me.*

Then glancing over at his desk, she saw the scattered pieces of paper: the fox story. She took up a page, her eyes darting over the words, and put it down. She turned to look at Tien Chen, a ripple of disquiet sweeping across her features. *You read it then, you know the story,* she said. *But it's not real, not a single word, it's all make-believe, mere fiction. He wrote it to make some sense of a story I told him once, but he didn't understand anything at all. He thinks it's about my life, but it's not. He thinks he knows who I am, but he doesn't, not a single thing.*

Yifan lay down beside Tien Chen, and pushed her back against him. They stayed like this for a long time. Her words, when she spoke, came to him as if from a deep well, from a different time. She told him a story.

The boy she loved when she was 15 was a classmate, someone whom she had known since she was a child. They were neighbours from the same kampung, and his parents had worked with hers in a fruit plantation. She and the boy had played in the rivers and fields of their kampung for as long as she could remember. To her, he was like one of her brothers—she had six of them—and she liked having him around as they climbed up the rambutan trees and fished in the shallow eddies of the river. He was a dark, lanky boy with long limbs and reminded her of an oversized monkey. She insisted on calling him Monkey Boy, a term of endearment that never failed to bring a grin to his face.

In retaliation, he had called her Wily Fox, for they and some friends had once spotted a large cat stalking among the pomelo trees at the fringe of the plantation and chased after it, scaring it into the thick underbrush. The last thing they had seen was a flick of its bushy tail as it slipped into the shrubs. In its wake, they saw a dead squirrel, a row of bite marks along its back, its neck snapped. They had not known then what the cat was—the only wild animals they had seen so far were small tribes of boars and monitor lizards—but the boy claimed it was a fox. He had seen a picture of one in an animal book, and was pretty sure every feature was exactly how he remembered it: light-brown pelt, pointy ears, triangular face. It could have been a wild dog, she said, but by then, most of them had agreed with the boy: it was a fox, it's definitely a fox.

So when the boy called her a fox, all Yifan could think of was the thick luxurious coat of the fox, the glimpses she had caught as the animal fled from them, darting between the trees. She remembered the tight graceful spring in its legs as it stretched out the length of its body, leaping away in fright. She had not minded being called a fox: a nimble, refined, beautiful creature, in her eyes. The name was stuck to her and became a pet name, even after they outgrew their childhood and stumbled headlong into adolescence.

It was during this hazy period of studies and hormones and monthly periods that Yifan became aware of her feelings for the boy, who was transforming in slow, fixed stages before her eyes: the jump in height, the shadow of a stubble above his lips and chin, the sprouting of hair on his thin arms and legs. He remained tall and lanky, and when he turned 15, he was already a head taller than Yifan. They had always got along well; he had an even temperament, gentle and good-natured, which, along with his odd sense of humour, was what had drawn Yifan to him.

Yet, despite his warm, genial front, Yifan also noticed a dark, moody streak that ran alongside his more personable self, occasionally rearing its head in a sudden gesture of annoyance, a turn of phrase or a long bout of silence. She was quick to notice his change of moods, able to read them well, and because of this, he often turned to her for advice and companionship. Yifan was naturally happy with the attention Monkey Boy was giving her, though she was hesitant about making her affection known. For one thing, he was reticent about sharing his feelings with her, and over the years they had known each other she had never once heard him talk about his liking for anyone. She knew he was innately shy—never one to make the first move—but she had seen him with the other girls in the class, and it was evident that he was well-liked by a few of them.

Because of their close friendship, many thought they

were a couple, an assumption Yifan gave in to willingly, even secretly encouraged. But of course, the reality was far from the truth: Monkey Boy had never treated her as anything more than a confidante and considered their friendship as purely platonic, nothing more. Still, Yifan clung to the possibility of his returning her love one day, once she broke through his reticence.

After school, they would walk home together and often stop at the provision shop outside their kampung for Orange Fanta or Coke. There, he would chat with the shop owner, while Yifan stood beside him, her hand near to the boy's, pretending to study the packaging of sweets and peanut snacks on display. Sometimes, he would talk to the shop helper, a husky boy of 17, an ex-schoolmate who had dropped out to help out at his father's shop. Yifan joined in when they chatted, mostly about other schoolmates and teachers they knew and the movies they had caught in town over the weekend. Because the two boys used to play football in school, they shared a close camaraderie, which left Yifan out in the cold. But she was fine with it, since she could tell that Monkey Boy clearly enjoyed his interactions with this other boy, from how his face would light up with undiminished delight, and she enjoyed looking at him in this unfiltered state. When they left the shop, Monkey Boy would occasionally slip into a dreamy, distant mood, his thoughts far away. They would walk in companionable silence till they arrived at Yifan's house and he would wave and smile and walk away.

Some days, when Yifan felt a certain compulsion, she would secretly trail Monkey Boy. She knew he liked to take long walks on the fringe of the plantation, to a small clearing beside the silty river, and sensing his need for solitude, she never made her presence known to him. He often fell into long naps while lying on the riverbank, his arm flung across his eyes, and Yifan would dare herself to venture as close as she could without rousing him. She loved to watch him in repose, his vulnerability exposed, fragile and defenceless like a child; how she would like to reach out and touch him, on his forehead or chest, how her heart ached with a bewildering, terrifying longing. But instead she waited till he woke up, and fled the scene like a thief caught red-handed.

And then one day, she saw Monkey Boy with the provision shop helper at the clearing. They were talking, shoulders pressed together, and then Monkey Boy was touching the other's hands and face. Yifan's mind immediately went blank, cut off from her surroundings. The boys kissed and broke away from each other, their eyes alive with an incredulous fire. How was this possible? How had she not known?

Yifan was furious, stricken by a sense of forlornness and helplessness. She felt foolish and cheated and out of her depth.

She avoided Monkey Boy for a week—floating through the days like a headless being, drained of any thought—and then she wrote a short note to the other boy. She dropped it in his hand and left the provision shop before he could say anything. She heard nothing back from him. She observed Monkey Boy in class, wondering whether he knew about the note, but he revealed not a stitch of emotion.

Then at the start of the following week, he did not appear in school, and nobody knew why. After school, she was at his doorstep, and found out from his mother that he was "unwell". She asked for permission to see him, and upon entering his bedroom, she saw the bandage on his wrist. The sight of it hit her right in the gut, and knocked the air out of her. She'd done this to him, the boy she loved. She was devastated. She had not imagined this outcome when she wrote the note; she had only wanted to warn the other boy, to shake them out of their stupor.

Sitting by the bedside beside his sleeping form, Yifan broke down. For days, she visited Monkey Boy after school, but he had not wanted to see her after her first visit. In desperation, she went to the other boy, who spoke curtly and firmly to her, telling her to stay away.

FOX FIRE GIRL

It was another week later when she heard the news: Monkey Boy had died. Slit his wrist again. Yifan wept.

That was when she started cutting herself, to feel the pain of what she had done. And when she finally had the chance, she decided to leave the kampung and head down to Singapore. She could not find a way to live there anymore. The blood of the boy was on her hands, and she had to live with it no matter what.

When she finished telling the story, Yifan rose from the bed and straightened her clothes. She turned to Tien Chen and smiled. She glanced at his bandaged hand, her expression wistful. *Now you know,* she said. *Please get well soon.*

She picked up the loose pages of the fox story and arranged them into a neat stack on the table. She put a hand on Tien Chen's forehead and heaved a sigh. Then she left the room, and disappeared from his life.

After his recovery, Tien Chen tried to look for Yifan, but she could not be found. At the kopitiam, he discovered that she had not turned up for work for several days. Her roommate told him that she had left after paying her share of the rent that month, and she didn't know where Yifan had gone. She left behind a cupboard full of clothes and belongings, only taking the small suitcase under the bed. Tien Chen brought everything back to his place, packed them into two medium-sized carton boxes he kept beside his wardrobe. For a long time, he did not touch the things in the boxes, or anything he had pilfered earlier. Yet he could not avoid the presence of these boxes in his bedroom; they spoke to him in their silence, wielding an immense weight within his mind.

Then one afternoon, unable to suppress his urges, he opened the boxes and disgorged their contents onto the floor. He arranged each piece of Yifan's belongings neatly, in piles and clusters, letting his hands linger on pieces he associated with a specific memory in his head. The memories came to him in short bursts: vivid at times, vague at others, pregnant with slippery, elusive meanings. What could he possibly do with these memories? They plagued him like a sickness he could not shake off, a fever that refused to break: the intimate smells of her body, the hair that fell across his chest like spools of dark threads, her cries during climax. Every fragment of Yifan continued to cling stubbornly to his mind, like shards of glass embedded in his skin; everything felt immeasurably stilted, ponderous.

When he was done sorting, Tien Chen gathered the piles and took them down to the burner-bin. He threw in her clothes first, which were quickly reduced to strips of fire before dying out. He kept feeding the fire, his mind focused solely on the task. The flames whipped and teased him unreservedly, but Tien Chen held back. The scab on his palm softened in the heat and started to itch. How long could he resist this time? He stood at the edge of the fire, hesitant, willing himself to stay still just for another moment. Soon, his hands were empty, and there was nothing left to burn. His mind had turned into a cell, bare and vacant.

The same night, he put the pages of the fox story into an envelope, and left for the man's flat. He went in the middle of the night; the air was cool and everything was quiet.

When he arrived at the man's doorstep, he noticed that the lights in the flat were still on, dim through the closed frosted windows. Tien Chen pressed his ear to the door, listening. He hoped to hear some sounds, perhaps Yifan's voice, but there was only silence. He had of course staked out the man's flat right after Yifan's disappearance, but she never appeared there. Did the man know he had been abandoned as well? Did he care? The thought of Yifan drew the breath out of him. Tien Chen slotted the envelope through the bottom slit of the door, and stood up. He could see the shadows trembling under the door.

Go, he told himself, *go now.*

But Tien Chen waited. He stood and waited, for a sign, for something to make him feel alive again.

GIRL

A VOICE CALLED out to her, soft and indistinct. Yifan had fallen asleep on the wicker chair, which she had dragged out of the living room and placed on the back porch of the family house. Upon opening her eyes, she gazed into the parade of trees bordering the old house. Was the voice from the dream, or did it come from somewhere in the forest? She listened, but heard nothing.

The evening light was subdued and amber around her, the air permeated with the raw resin smell of burnt wood. Yifan tried to trace the source of the burning, the wispy spirals of smoke rising in the distance. The familiar smell was a small, soothing comfort to her, a thing she remembered from the time she spent in the kampung a long time ago. A light breeze brought some relief, cooling her sweaty skin spotted with mosquito bites. She adjusted her damp T-shirt and glanced back into the kitchen, where she could see her mother busy at the stove, her figure bent to the task. How long had she slept? She put aside the old Chinese newspaper she had been reading and stood to stretch herself, her back and joints aching. The strain of the nine-hour bus journey had got to her.

Her mother had looked surprised when Yifan arrived at the doorstep early in the morning with a small suitcase, the same one she had used when she left Ipoh eight years ago. Yifan had not called to tell her mother that she was coming back; she had not expected to be leaving Singapore at such short notice. Three days before she decided to come back she had still been weighing her options; two nights before, restless in bed and unable to sleep, she had almost backed out of her decision. But still she had done it. And now she was here.

The family house was more run-down than she remembered. The zinc-panelled roof had corroded into a copper-red rust, and where there were holes, small attempts had been made to mend them with smears of plaster, resulting in unsightly patches of yellow and brown. The rafters were choked with thick threads of spiderwebs, lumpy with insect carcasses. Deep rot had settled into the wooden posts and beams of the house, darkening them with age spots and streaks. A thin fur of dust grew over every exposed surface, sometimes coalescing into small grey-skinned moulds and tails.

Yet everything else was almost how Yifan remembered it—the layout of the wooden furniture in the living room;

the row of nail-pegs beside the front door on which hung an assortment of discoloured plastic shopping bags; the soot-thickened, wood-fired stove. Even her old bedroom was left mostly intact: the chipped-at-the-edges vanity table, the peeling green linoleum floor, the grime-covered sparrow windchime. Only her mother lived here now; Yifan's father had passed away years ago, and all her siblings had moved out to different states: to Kuala Lumpur, Penang and Johor Bahru, where they had found jobs or gotten married. If Yifan had wanted to, she would have felt each of their absences sharply, but she remained wary of such feelings of nostalgia and sentimentality. People moved on, and people coped—just as she and her mother had. Nothing stayed the same for long, not even family.

Yifan discovered small traces of her old life in odd and unexpected spaces in the bedroom. She found the torn satchel bag she had used in secondary school, still pinned with a fading Snoopy button, buried behind a carton box of used textbooks and Chinese romance novels. Inside she found a journal that contained a ragged pencil drawing. The fox-girl. A memory came immediately to her, along with a name: Peng Soon. Yifan held the image of his face—sketchy, with dissolving features—briefly in her mind, before she slotted the drawing back into the journal.

In a photo album filled with old school photographs, Yifan saw her almost unrecognisable younger self, her straight black hair clipped just above her shoulders, her skin deeply tanned. She was 15 then, beaming with her classmates, holding up a Happy Teachers' Day banner. Her eyes sought out the familiar faces, and immediately she spotted Peng Soon—his narrow face, side-parted hair, and lanky frame. For a moment, she wondered where he was now—still living in Ipoh perhaps?

In thinking about him, her mind pulled out yet another loose memory: Hai Feng.

• • •

When times were unbearable, Yifan would recall the words of her mother: *Eat your sorrow.* Three simple words she took great comfort in; words that never failed to lift her spirits when she was feeling down. She remembered the first time her mother whispered these words to her while trying to calm her down. Yifan was 10 years old, and had been whipped by her father for secretly stealing and smoking his cigarettes. Since then she had pulled these words out of her memory on many occasions, especially during the hard times when she transitioned from adolescence to adulthood, from Ipoh to Singapore.

By nature, Yifan had a cheerful, well-adjusted disposition, and rarely gave herself to long bouts of melancholy or sadness. She knew, of course, the ways that the world could break or change a person, permanently and indefinitely, but she had always been adaptive to such forces, having learnt from a young age to change herself in order not to succumb to things that were beyond her control. She had her share of hardships, and was wary of taking on another's. What did she know about another person's life or circumstances, and what could she possibly do to effect real change? It wasn't up to her.

Still, she liked to listen to other people's tales, and it seemed enough to just listen, to bear witness to their stories. People were very willing to talk about their lives if you gave them half a chance, pouring their hearts out as if the act of telling these stories was as vital as eating or breathing. Everyone had something they wanted to say about their lives. People seemed to want to wrap every moment of their existence within the skin of a story, with a beginning, middle and ending, neat and tidy and predictable, as if their lives could be sequenced to pattern by will. Every experience could yield a seed that could flourish into a fully-grown tree, into a story ripe for telling.

Yifan had listened to enough stories throughout her young life to wear a person's heart out, but she had never allowed them to become more than just stories. They were a jumble of things both made-up and real—facts, imagination, fantasy, memories—and nothing more. Stories are stories, she told herself, you make of them what you will, and that's all there is. She thought that the truth of a story lay in the listener's belief in the storyteller, and Yifan believed in the stories she had been told the same way she believed in Monarch butterflies, or a forest fire ravaging some distant land—as something real and plausible, but also fleeting, out of reach.

In thinking about stories, Yifan often wondered which were the ones she wanted to remember about her own life. Where should she begin? She could not put her finger on which events marked the point in her life where things really started to matter. Her childhood in Ipoh? Her schooling days? Maybe an episode involving her family?

Start from your earliest memory, someone told her once, the one you cannot forget, even now. But what was her earliest memory? She had an old photo she still kept with her: she as a baby, sitting on a rattan chair in a white singlet, staring vacantly into space. What did she know about the child in the photo from the features that had long disappeared from her own face, the fat cheeks, a button-nub of a nose? The photo had been taken when she was two, something her parents did for each of their nine children—a rare investment of time and money, given how poor they were back then. She had taken the photo with her when she left Ipoh, one of the few mementoes she kept from a period of time she did not remember any more.

Could memories be substituted with stories then, she wondered, as the means through which the mind worked, breaking each experience down to a handful of images, and building it up again as a loose stream of narration? Yifan knew it was easy to confuse story and memory, to differentiate between what really happened with what was fabricated. People always wanted more from their lives, and when they didn't get it, they would make something up as a way of redemption, a means of escape. Yifan understood this well. She, too, had made up her life in as many ways as she could think of, to give it the varied shades it lacked, to provide her with the cover under which she could make her own escape.

When Yifan listened to the stories of others, she cared little about how they were told, or what they would reveal about the person telling them. She was more interested in being within the story she was listening to, in order to exist in that state created by the storytelling: pure senses, immaterial. Immersed in these stories, she could shake the skin off her very self, and take up that of others.

When she was younger, she used to get scared by the idea of living in another skin, seeing everything with new eyes, and feeling things that were not hers. How much of herself would she have to give up to imagine the death and pain and sadness of others? How much would she gain? Sometimes, when someone's story had truly got to her, Yifan would wander through her days unfocused and unhinged, her mind snapping in and out of various daydreams.

Her mother used to chide her for always being lost in her own world, not seeing where she was going or doing. *But where else could I be,* she wanted to say, *except inside my head?* Even if she was lost, Yifan knew she was lost in a tight, private place inside her that only she knew, a place forever sealed off from other people. A sanctuary, and also a gaol, of her own creation. It was a space she guarded staunchly.

Yifan often found remembering her own past an exasperating, even tedious act. When she made a deliberate effort to recall events from her past, she would draw up snippets from her memory that were vague and disjointed; yet sometimes when she was preoccupied with a task, her mind would suddenly spin a contiguous reel of a near-forgotten episode that she could neither make head nor tail of. Why that particular memory, she often puzzled, and was there any significance to it? Had she unconsciously brought it up?

She often tried to ascribe some meaning to each recollection. Perhaps she was feeling lonely and thinking of home, or maybe craving affirmation or recognition. She needed to know that there was logic to it, something inherently coherent and rational about how one thing connected to another. It took some time for her to realise the fallacy of that belief. There was no way to bridge what she thought she knew with what had actually happened in the past, caught in the constant flux between wanting to remember and the desire to forget.

To Yifan, her past was quicksand that swallowed everything in sight, and in order to gain proper footing, she needed to give herself something to hold on to, a structure that could stand on its own. So she constructed her own past out of all the fragments she could remember, and in doing so mastered it, like a wild beast on a leash. She would tell her own story in whatever way she wanted, and every part of it would be true and unequivocal and valid. Her past became something pliable and malleable, something she could mould into any shape or form she desired, to add to or subtract from or fatten by her own effort, with her imagination. In this way she freed herself of her past and the murk of her own history.

As a young girl, Yifan knew enough to hide behind her words, to present a front to the people around her. It was not something that was intentional at first, though it gradually took on the permanence of a screen, to block out unwanted meddling or questions. When her friends commented on the old ugly school bag she'd had since she started primary school, she told them that her parents were simply too busy with work to buy her a new one (it was a hand-me-down from an older sister; they could not afford a new bag for her); when they saw the scars on her arms and legs, she said she had accidentally fallen into a thorny shrub on her way home after being chased by a wild kampung dog (her father had a savage, unpredictable temper when he drank, which everyone in the family was acutely attuned to, though it did nothing to prevent the beatings).

School constantly presented her with tests that she had to find ways to manoeuvre around; every question about her family was deflected with a blank or neutral reply, one that invited no further follow-up. Yifan knew her family was poor; her parents were fruit plantation workers, and their meagre combined income was barely enough to feed a brood of nine children. It was a fact so ingrained in her psyche that it was as incontrovertible as the shape of her eyes or the length of her fingers. It had not bothered her, though she had seen on several occasions the pitying glances from her classmates; she wanted more than anything to never feel she lacked anything, to be reduced to an object of such vain and pitiless judgement.

Outwardly, Yifan cultivated an easy, submissive demeanour, one that drew people to her. But inwardly, she had shaped herself into someone who had learnt not to leave anything to chance, to hold people at bay no matter how friendly or accommodating they were towards her. She kept her smile on all the time and was always quick to offer a reply, a reason or an excuse. Her classmates came to trust her and to tell her their stories, and it was in the role of a confidante that she knew she had an upper hand, that she could make people feel indebted to her. Yifan listened closely to her classmates, not because she was interested in them or their lives, but to look out for signs of weakness, for their inconstancies and follies. She promised to keep their secrets, to say not a word. And when there was a need for some form of reciprocity, to keep their friendship in balance, Yifan would spin something from the random dregs of her life and, after telling it with sufficient earnestness, would swear the other person to secrecy.

Yet, back at home, Yifan was a completely different creature all together. She withdrew into herself amid the noisy, overwhelming bustle of her family, like a rodent slipping back into a hole, seeking safety. She took up her prescribed role of mousey sister and obedient daughter. As the youngest child out of six boys and three girls, her parents did not expect much out of her, just as long as she stayed out of trouble, and out of sight. She kept under the radar and rarely made herself visible. When her siblings got into fights with one another, she would choose not to take sides, feigning disinterest or indifference. Growing up, her two older sisters often teased Yifan and reminded her that she was an accident, that their parents had not wanted any more children but were very careless ("*And too poor to get rid of you,*" one had whispered under her breath, meanly), and so they'd had no choice but to have her.

Sometimes, in her daydreams, Yifan wondered what she would be if she wasn't born—would she be a soul without a body, waiting somewhere to be reaped for life, or would she be nothing, a void that did not exist? What would that be like? Yifan closed her eyes and tried to imagine herself not-existing, to strip her mind clean of any consciousness. But it was impossible to do so; even the emptiness that lay behind her closed eyelids was weighted with an irresistible force, pulling her back into the fixed, unyielding confines of her body.

If there was any consolation to her childhood, it was Yifan's mother. Demure and diminutive, her mother was a shaky, unsure shadow against the bigger, more menacing presence of Yifan's father. Perhaps it was the luck of being the youngest; her mother doted on her the most, even when she was stretched to a breaking point by the constant demands and badgering from the older children.

When her mother got a day off from work and they were alone, Yifan would crawl into her lap as the latter sat and split the watermelon seeds between her teeth and told her stories. Most of the time, Yifan could not understand or follow the thread of the stories, especially when they were about her mother's past—distant relatives she had never heard of, and places and events that seemed to exist in a different time. But when they were tales about animals, and sometimes people, her ears would prick up: the ancient tortoise that transformed itself into an island to save a band of shipwrecked sailors, the friendships between a snake and a girl, a wolf and a shepherd, the wise elephant that travelled a thousand kilometres to summon the rain. In the tales that involved people—mostly children—Yifan would imagine herself not as the hapless, helpless humans who could not save their skins even if they wanted to, but as the wise animals that often intervened in the nick of time, to offer assistance, and to give fully of themselves. Their sacrifices and their transformations—always permanent, always irreversible—often seemed wild and grand in Yifan's eye, compared to the inconsequential, feeble actions of the humans. She wondered whether any of the animals would have done anything differently if they had another choice. Often, she would fall asleep in her mother's lap as she turned over these details in her mind: island, fur, scales, relentless rain. Her mother's storytelling continued long into Yifan's childhood, and when it finally stopped, these stories had already taken root in her, sinking into dark, fertile soil.

A childhood story Yifan remembered: in a village, there was a fox who was a vegetarian, because of his beliefs. The other foxes were at first fascinated with his dietary decision, but gradually came to ignore him, treating him as an eccentric, an outcast. The vegetarian-fox did not mind what the others thought of him, and was more than happy to go his own way, and eat whatever was growing in the forest behind the village: durian, pomelo, mangosteen, guava, starfruit. He was able to make many new friends among the other animals, now that he wasn't hunting them. But he was often hungry, even though he always ate his fill of fruits at every meal.

One day, one of his new friends, a squirrel, came to him and presented him with a nut. "I know you have been losing weight. So I want to give you this nut that I've been keeping for a special occasion," said the squirrel. The fox politely refused, but the squirrel insisted, thrusting the nut into the fox's paws. "Eat it, and you'll know why it's so special," the squirrel added.

The fox waited for his squirrel friend to leave before he cracked the nut open and ate the flesh inside. He chewed softly and swallowed and waited for something to happen. His stomach felt light and airy as usual, emptied out. And then suddenly he felt it: the slow throbs of a growing pain. He started to shiver and scratch himself all over. His thick fur fell out in patches, and his skin constricted. He felt himself shrinking, becoming smaller and smaller. When the shivering finally subsided, the fox ran over to the river, anxious and nearly out of his mind. He peeked into the water and saw his new reflection. He had transformed into a squirrel! And he could not be happier. He ran back to his village in his excitement, wanting to tell the others the good news, but the moment he entered it, one of his neighbours, an elderly scholarly fox with a monocle, jumped on him and ate him alive.

Yifan recalled chuckling at the end of the story when she first heard it. Her mother smiled and stroked her face and hair. *Don't be like the fox in his foolishness,* her mother said. *You don't have to go around telling people everything that has happened to you, whether it's good or bad. It's good enough you alone know; you don't have to share everything with everyone, you hear?* Yifan nodded in blind assent, even as she was still trying to wrap her head around the story.

While Yifan's mother was able to shelter her from much of what was happening in the family, there were still things that Yifan could not help but notice. Because her parents worked side by side throughout the day in the fruit plantation, they were silent around each other at home, each tending privately to his or her own tasks, him with his newspapers and repairs around the house, her with her cooking and cleaning. If they had something to say to the other, they would relay the message through one of the children, who would pass it along. Because she was always in close proximity to her mother, Yifan was often asked to relay messages to her father. To approach him, Yifan had to summon a certain amount of courage in order not to stammer or trip over her words. Her father barely acknowledged her sometimes, and would dismiss her impatiently with a quick word or a toss of his hand even before she was done with the message.

Yifan never knew what made her parents stay together despite their apparent differences (her father's quick temper, her mother's passivity, their mutual indifference); if one had shown the other any act of kindness or love, Yifan never saw it. Once, late at night, when she was 11, lying on a mattress, she heard muffled noises coming from her parents' bed. Raising her head, she stared at the moving mass under the thin blanket, and for a brief moment, she thought her father was hitting her mother again, something that occurred with a dogged regularity whenever he drank too much or lost money at the weekly gambling game in town. But the noise she heard was different, one that did not quite sound like a person in distress. Then moments later, when Yifan saw the rise and fall of her parents' bodies, she sank back onto the mattress, pulled the blanket over her head and closed her eyes, her throat thickening with balls of spit.

When Yifan sensed that the movements on the bed finally died down, she heard her mother getting up and walking softly out of the bedroom. Yifan crept out from under the blanket a few seconds later and trailed her mother. Stationing herself in a dark corner of the kitchen, with a half-obscured view of the toilet with the door ajar, Yifan watched her mother clean up with a damp rag. In the harsh, fluorescent light of the toilet, her mother's body looked worn and saggy, interlocking varicose veins streaking across the broad flanks of her thighs, green and red and black like thick threads, her breasts with dark-ringed aureoles drooping heavy and useless. Yifan crossed her arms as the pinched nubs of flesh on her chest ached, feeling oddly shamed but also thrilled for what was happening to her body. She'd had her first period just three months ago, and was aware of similar changes occurring in her classmates: tight white singlets to hide the budding growth of the breasts, faint wisps of hair in their armpits, the fleshing-out of hips and buttocks. Her classmates were open and candid about these changes, and Yifan paid careful attention to what they were saying, mentally ticking off any changes they had against hers. She was also keenly aware of the stares of some of her male classmates that stayed a beat longer on her body, as if they were attempting to pick it apart to find something they weren't sure of themselves. Hunching her shoulders and keeping her eyes low, Yifan made every effort to stay in the background; she needed the space and privacy to understand what her body was doing, even though the understanding was slow and often muddled, inadequate.

Studying her mother washing up in the toilet, Yifan could see how time had worked its fingers through her body, turning it soft in some parts, and coarse in others. The stretch marks below her abdomen, the sad hanging lump of her stomach, her wide, fleshy hips—they hid a different story from what was exposed, visible to the eyes: her mother's taut brown arms, her toned legs, her kind, weathered face. How many stories would a woman's body tell over time, and which was the one that mattered?

In her own changing body, Yifan felt the same doubts running through her, pulling her in opposite directions. She recalled what her mother had told her when she had her first period: *you're no longer a child now, your body is changing, and you have to know what it needs.* Yifan, lying dazed on the bed and knotted with the newfound pain, could only think of the unreasonableness of what was happening to her, which had felt personal, unequivocal and unfair. Why her, why the pain—and for how long, she bemoaned foolishly then.

Looking at the pale, wrinkled skin of her mother's stomach, Yifan could not imagine the fact of her birth, nor that of her siblings'. Nine births, nine months each time; nearly eight years of her mother's life, laden with the complicated burdens of pregnancy, each taking something out of her.

Even while the heft of her mother's body had thickened over the years, a great part of her seemed to have hollowed out.

When her mother stooped to rinse the rag, Yifan caught a glimpse of the wild, unruly bush of her pubic hair, and unable to watch any further, fumbled her way back to the mattress, willing herself not to think about the things which she had no means to understand fully, or escape from.

In time, Yifan's body began to fill out, giving her a definition and form that was permanent, undeniable. I'm becoming a woman, she would think to herself. *I'm no longer a girl, I'm becoming something else, something more.* She carried the new weight of her body with as much grace and intuition as she could muster. She took comfort in the fact that all her female classmates were experiencing the same changes, even as she faltered from time to time in her grasp of the new and pressing needs of her own body. She could sense her mind branching out from its restricted confines, feeling its ways into the lives of others, teasing out what lay beyond the smiling, shiny surfaces.

Especially her male classmates. They were a species unto themselves, and she was secretly fascinated by their world, which came with its own rules and laws and gravity. She watched them with a fervid intent that bordered on the maniacal, which she had learnt to mask in degrees with lowered, sideways glances and a cool detachment. Unlike her female classmates, who revelled in heated closed-door discussions of the boys in their cohort—who they liked, who they found charming or offensive, who they wanted as boyfriends—Yifan remained stolidly mum about who she had taken a fancy to. When pressed, she would state the overwhelmingly obvious choice, a boy who was a favourite among her classmates: Hai Feng, a tall, lean boy with a smooth, angular face, captain of the school badminton team, already destined for future greatness in the national squad. It was much easier than if she had to name the person she had set her eyes on and defend her choice.

The person in question was a classmate who sat two rows in front of her: a quiet, reserved boy who liked to sketch in a spiral notebook during the lull between classes. Peng Soon had a spidery frame, long arms and legs, with a closely-shaven head and small, high-set ears. Looking at him in profile over the course of six months in Secondary Two, Yifan had longed to trace her finger along the austere lines of his jaws and nose, to feel the stubble on his sharp chin. When she was called out by the teachers to come to the front of the classroom—to write the answers of an algebra problem on the chalkboard, or to present a book report—she would take the narrow aisle skirting past his desk so that he would have no choice but to look up at her. They had only exchanged a few words on occasion, mostly about deadlines for homework or remedial classes after school, and she had not dared to approach him for anything specific.

For some time, Yifan assumed her interest in Peng Soon was purely platonic and observational. Then almost overnight, it became an unwavering point of fixation, commanding her attention like an insistent, silent beacon. This rude flourishing of an urgent and unappeasable feeling inside her was strange and foreign, and she did not trust herself enough to give in to it just yet, so Yifan was cautious and reticent, keeping her distance. When the other girls talked about Peng Soon, they did so in broad, generalising strokes—"*too dorky*", "*too serious*", "*so stiff*"—and labelled him, unkindly, as The Artist, goading one another to model for him, to be the subject of his masterpieces. Yifan listened, but rarely participated in her classmates' taunting, refusing to give them anything they could use against her.

During the half-hour of recess, Yifan would see Peng Soon sitting on the cement bench beside the school field under the shade of a casuarina tree, his body bent over a page, busily sketching. He had never shown his drawings to anyone in class, but Yifan found out from the classmate who sat next to him that Peng Soon was always sketching strange creatures that made no sense whatsoever.

At one long afternoon assembly in the school hall, Yifan feigned a stomach ache and sneaked back to the classroom. She rifled through Peng Soon's bag and took out his notebook. It was filled with pencil drawings of animals with fantastical features: a winged leopard with two pairs of hairy legs, a three-horned eagle with the face of an elf, a bespectacled moth with a slick, iron-clad body of a fighter plane. The pages were slightly warped from constant erasing and scribbling.

Yifan paused and held her breath at one of the drawings: a human-sized fox (or was it a woman?) with bare breasts and pointy ears, a trail of thick fur lining the contours of her body, a bushy tail in mid-swing. In her paws, the fox was holding something—a burning orb of fire? A half-eaten heart? Something shifted inside Yifan's head, dislodging a strip of memory—had she dreamt this before? Why was the creature so familiar? She tore the page out and stuffed it into the pocket of her school pinafore and returned the notebook to the bag. If Peng Soon discovered the missing page later on, he did not let on. Yifan kept the page in the folds of her diary and hid it deep inside a cupboard, underneath a pile of old T-shirts.

During recess, the girls from Yifan's class would sit at

the edge of the field and watch the boys play soccer while gossiping. Liu Ying, the queen bee of Yifan's clique, turned to Yifan while they were playing their usual round of Truth or Dare, and asked: *Now, your turn. Would you rather kiss the snail or Hai Feng?* The other girls bent to hear what Yifan had to say, exchanging openly eager looks. Yifan knew the answer she ought to give, yet she hesitated momentarily, looking away for good measure.

In that split second, Liu Ying sensed the opportunity for a round of ribbing and yelped: *Oh my god, you want to kiss Hai Feng, right? You always want to kiss him, I know. You want him as a boyfriend, right? You slut, you cheap slut.*

The girls rallied around Liu Ying's mock-outburst and chimed in with more insults, laughing. Yifan, caught off-guard, could only feign ignorance and playfully plead innocence. Later, returning to their classroom, they saw Hai Feng coming from the opposite direction and started laughing again, pushing Yifan to the front of the group. *Go, go, your prince charming is coming for you. Go kiss him.*

Hai Feng glanced over at them and gave a puzzled smile, his stare fixed on Yifan. Breaking from the girls, Yifan ran back to the classroom, her face a radiant foil of heat and embarrassment. She could not process a single thought throughout the rest of the lessons that morning. The teasing continued the next day, and spread to the students from the other classes. Most of the teasing was harmless, and Yifan was quick to brush it aside.

Yet the discomfort of being at the centre of all the bloated attention gnawed at her, as if she had accidentally exposed herself with a small indiscretion, and she was worried that Peng Soon would get wind of it. During lessons, she cast nervous looks at him, and once, as she was slipping into one of her daydreams, Peng Soon turned around and gave her a—knowing?—smile. Yifan felt suddenly and painfully visible, blood rushing to her face.

Yifan did very little the next few days except to shift the attention away from her. The excitement soon passed. But just when she thought the matter was all settled and forgotten, she was approached by Hai Feng as she was walking home from school one afternoon. He tapped her on the shoulder and called out her name; Yifan wondered whether he had known it at all before the incident. He asked whether she was taking a bus to the town centre. Yifan, looking up at the towering figure before her, spoke slowly after a long moment. *No, I'm going home,* she said, aware of the glances that were coming her way from the other students.

Before Hai Feng could say another word, a trio of boys came up and slapped him on the head. *Whoa, you dirty bastard, what are you doing? Trying to woo this girl ah,* one of them shouted. Hai Feng punched the guy lightly on the shoulder, breaking into laughter, which the other boys quickly joined in. Yifan, sensing the gap in the tight situation, turned and ran all the way to the next street corner, feeling the scorching eyes of the boys on her back.

The next time Hai Feng came up to her, Yifan was more prepared, having worked out the right way to respond. The previous encounter was a disaster; this time, she had decided to present the same well-worn public self that she used with the girls in her clique: affable, accommodating, armed with an easy smile. When their eyes met, Yifan noticed that Hai Feng's eyes were not entirely black, more of a dark hazel. There was a steely canny pull in them which Yifan tried to extract herself from by glancing away several times.

Have you tried the new dessert shop, the one that sells durian cendol? he asked. Yifan shook her head. *Do you want to go this Saturday? If you are free, I mean.*

Though she had never been asked out on a date before, Yifan paused for a good moment, as if deliberating her decision, before finally nodding her head. *Why not, sounds good,* she said.

On Saturday, Yifan hurried through her chores of sweeping and mopping the house. She gave her mother the excuse that she needed to go to a classmate's house to do a group project; she could not tell her mother who she was seeing just yet. To bring Hai Feng up would mean having to offer the backstory of the teasing, which hardly justified what she was doing. She thought she would mention him to her mother later, when things were more settled.

Theirs was a small town, and everyone knew where everyone else lived. Though Hai Feng had offered to meet Yifan at the road junction down the alley where she lived, she chose to meet him at the bus stop beside the row of shophouses where the dessert shop was located. Hai Feng was already waiting when she arrived, holding a small plastic bag of mangosteens. *For you,* he said.

Hai Feng's father owned a provision shop near their school, and since Yifan often had to run to the shop to buy packs of smokes or bottles of soy sauce for her parents, she was familiar with his family background. But Hai Feng rarely helped out at the provision shop, since he was also the youngest, and there were already two older siblings to assist in the daily running of the shop. *The boy ah, busier than me, always at one of his badminton practices,* his father used to complain to Yifan whenever he saw her, though his tone was more proud than chiding.

At the dessert shop, Hai Feng guided Yifan to an empty

table, putting his hand lightly on the small of her back. Though it was only a little gesture, Yifan could feel the heat emanating from the touch, coming through the fabric of her beige blouse. She let Hai Feng order the dessert, deferring to his choices; she did not have a sweet tooth, and would have preferred something savoury. But she did not feel it was the right time to state her preferences. Since the days of her childhood, she had learnt to go along with other people's choices if the decision or outcome had little or no significant consequence to her. So what if she had to give in for just that moment—it would not kill her, anyway.

When they were done with the desserts, they went over to the nearby shopping mall and walked around aimlessly before Yifan had to leave. On the bus, Hai Feng touched the side of her hand, and Yifan did not pull away.

It was on the next date that they held hands, and on their fifth one that they kissed. She knew a kiss was forthcoming, inevitable, and she had prepared for it beforehand by kissing the back of her hand as well as a toy bear from her childhood for several nights. Yet she was still surprised by the force of that first kiss. The close, intimate smell of Hai Feng; his tongue touching hers, overeager and writhing like a slug in her mouth.

She was the one to break away from the kiss, feeling out

of breath, unable to find a footing for her rampant thoughts. *Are you okay?* Hai Feng asked. Yifan could only nod. In the few seconds of the kiss, she had felt a divide opening up inside her, splitting her in half—a child suspended in time inside her, and now something that wasn't quite completely formed yet, a creature only just starting to flex its new limbs, testing new boundaries. She had taken the first big leap— and it seemed like it was impossible to bridge that first gap of experience except by hurling herself fully into it.

Now that she was here on the other side, she felt lost. What did the kiss mean? And where could she go from now on? She felt loose and untethered in the hide of her new skin, unable to lock herself into the same places in her head or heart. She glanced at Hai Feng's face as he leant in for a longer and deeper kiss. There was nothing there for her to read, neither recognition nor confirmation. She kissed him back, forcibly and unwaveringly, as if to push away her fears, to make the moment truer than it actually felt.

That night, still in the grip of the kisses' enchantment, Yifan slipped out of the house and walked into the forest on a well-trodden path that led to the river. Moonlight painted the forest interior with a weak bluish luminescence, and as she walked, Yifan listened for any sudden noise or movement in her surroundings. Moving through the cool, light air of the night, Yifan turned her vision inwards, her mind filled with images she was trying to work into a coherent sequence.

As she came closer to the river, she heard a burst of movement in a thicket of bushes on her right. She stopped and kept herself very still. In a small pale pool of moonlight, she saw a flash of something—fur, tail?—scampering and burrowing itself into the thick underbrush. She remained motionless for long seconds.

When the sound finally faded away, Yifan picked up her pace and broke into a small clearing beside the gurgling river. She walked to the edge and listened to the gushing flow of the water, thinking about the stories her mother had told her of the forest, its dangers and also of its secrets. She allowed these stories—of capricious forest-bound creatures and their flighty pacts of love and revenge—to soothe her nerves, to calm her down. How like them she was, in her appetites, in her fretfulness and longings. The longer she stood there, the more she began to lose the sense of who she was, as if the night were slowly breaking down the perimeter of her body, absorbing her into a bigger, darker unknown. As the air cooled her skin and her eyes began to grow weary, Yifan lay on the damp grass and looked up into the curved dome of the night sky. Her thoughts became softer, more pliable. Before she could even think of fighting it, Yifan had fallen right into a deep, barren sleep.

Shortly after that night Yifan approached Peng Soon during recess and asked to look at his drawings. He did not seem surprised by her request, as if he had been waiting for someone to ask him all along. Yifan had been sitting with the other girls on the stone benches in the school garden, and when one of them saw Peng Soon under the tree and made a curt offhand remark, Yifan got up and made a mock declaration. *Let me see what the great artist is drawing,* she told the girls, playfully fluttering her eyelids. Everyone broke out in giggles, jeering and egging her on. Yifan had needed something to push her into action, something she could use to disguise her own agenda, a cover of sorts. As she moved away from the group, she steeled her nerves, afraid that if she thought any further about her initial decision her fear would grow too strong and she would back out of it.

Everything had been progressing smoothly with Hai Feng, and while she would have liked to slow it down so her mind could come around to what was happening—her fledgling emotions, the new sensations—it had seemed impossible. Though they kept their courtship under wraps, she was certain that they were now a couple; with the hand-holding and kissing, what else could they be? Things were falling quickly into place, yet Yifan felt caged in and overwhelmed. There were other feelings, like those for Peng Soon, that she could not resolve or push aside. It felt like time was running out for her, as though the next step she took with Hai Feng would seal her in a bind that she would not be able to get out of unscathed. She needed to do something, anything to break out of the fear.

Peng Soon tilted the drawing pad towards her, and Yifan bent low to look at it. There was a faint sketching of a bull-man with a muscular body covered in snake tattoos. *Is that you?* Yifan asked.

Peng Soon chuckled and flipped the page, and began to draw several dark lines across it. *Hold still. Let me see you clearly,* he said.

Yifan sat immobile, holding her posture rigid, and watched as Peng Soon's hand moved deftly across the page. She liked his long, slender fingers, which were soft, almost feminine.

For the next few days, she sat for him as he drew, swinging between states of anxiety and equanimity. They talked throughout the sessions, and Yifan was happy to let Peng Soon take the lead in the conversations. He seldom spoke about himself or his life, but instead directed questions at Yifan, enquiring about her hobbies and studies, her family.

When something in her replies caught his interest, he would glance up from the page, a half-smile teasing the corners of his lips. During classes, she noticed Peng Soon turning to look at her more than usual. Each time that happened, she would feel a jolt like a static charge, quickening her senses. When Peng Soon gave her the final drawing of her portrait, Yifan took the opportunity to ask him out as a way of thanking him. Peng Soon registered a moment of puzzlement, before agreeing in the next breath.

They went out on a Saturday with no plans for what they wanted to do or see; they simply walked around the shopping mall for an hour and sat down for a round of bubble tea when they were tired. Yifan was not afraid of bumping into Hai Feng as she knew he was busy with his badminton training for the next three weeks, preparing for an upcoming regional tournament. As far as she was aware, Hai Feng had not caught on to what she was doing. Nobody in their mutual social circles knew they were a couple yet, since they did not give each other undue attention in school. It was an unspoken mutual agreement between them; for Yifan, it meant that she could still test her feelings for Hai Feng, to find out what she really wanted.

So, after that first outing, Yifan went out on several other occasions with Peng Soon—to the movies, to the games arcade, to the bookshop. Watching their third movie together, Yifan sneaked her hand into Peng Soon's, and he held it in his lap. While Hai Feng's grip was firm and clammy, Peng Soon's was soft and loose.

In this and other ways, Yifan started making comparisons between them. One was intense and passionate, the other was cool and obliging. One loved the outdoors and long walks in nature, the other preferred air-conditioned environs and an unhurried pace; both had strong, good appetites, for food, for new discoveries, for experimentation. One kissed lightly on the lips, brushing his skin gently against her, the other searched the interior of her mouth with his tongue, leaving her lips sore and tender at times. She felt differently for each of them, varying only by degree and magnitude and situation, and even then, her feelings were fluid, changing from one day to another. At any given point in time, she would prefer one over the other, but in the next moment, she would change her mind. When Yifan was with one, she had to make a conscious effort not to think about the other, though sometimes she would mix up something one said with the other. Small innocuous stuff that she was thankfully quick in masking or diverting away from, quelling any unnecessary suspicion.

The busy secret life she lived, dating two boys at the same

time, was not one she would have chosen for herself. But in the thick of it, she did not want to think too much about what it meant or where it was going—whether it was right or wrong or something else altogether. Yifan only knew she liked the two boys, and to give one or the other up was something she was not ready to do, not just yet. She liked the fact that she was someone who could be loved in very specific and very different ways by two different persons, and all that she had to do was to present herself in a different light to each of them, to remake herself to fit what they thought she was. Wasn't that what everyone else was doing—to reinvent themselves for the sake of love, to change themselves for the better? And what was wrong with that?

One of the ways Yifan gave of herself was through her body. At 15, her body had long shed the bony, formless shape of a child, and taken on the defining form and proportions of a woman—full breasts, a trim waist, generous hips. She was well aware of the impressions her body made on the imaginations of Hai Feng and Peng Soon, and the demands they required of her. She was not squeamish or ignorant of her own body's needs, and because of that, she was willing to give in in order to meet these needs.

When Hai Feng first touched her breasts, she did not resist, and when Peng Soon did it later on, she merely closed her eyes and leant forward submissively. With the urgency and clumsiness of first-timers, they fumbled through the unthinking, uneasy stages of lust for some sort of release, and Yifan was quick to discover her role in mastering what the boys had no control over—their lack of restraint, their bodily need for climax. When they were in the spell of their own lust, they reverted to larger, needier, more cumbersome versions of themselves, ones which hungered for everything in sight, seizing whatever they could lay their hands on. It was something that seemed almost childlike to Yifan, like boys with their toys and their bloated declarations of strength and abilities.

Still, Yifan was not unaware of what she also needed. To get them attuned to her demands, she sometimes withheld her enthusiasm or feigned a lack of interest. The boys would usually catch on to her moods, and because they were not callous or heedless, they were always eager to redeem themselves, and bring Yifan around. They did everything they could to please her, and Yifan was more than willing to play her role, to indulge them.

In all her dealings with Hai Feng and Peng Soon, Yifan was careful not to be seen with one or the other too prominently. Thus, miraculously, throughout the four months she was secretly seeing both of them, neither saw her in public with the other. While the town they lived in wasn't exactly small, it had enough breadth and hidden spaces for them to slip into. For her dates with Hai Feng, she chose the movies, where they could hold hands discreetly; in any case, they were not given to showy displays of affection in public, since Hai Feng was the school badminton captain and needed to maintain his public image. With Peng Soon, they stuck to window-shopping at the malls (no hand-holding) and visits to the bookshops and art supplies stores before heading back to Peng Soon's, where he had a room of his own. There, he would show her his latest drawings and they would lie on his bed, talking and sometimes kissing.

Unlike Hai Feng, who took every opportunity when they were alone to initiate the kissing and touching, Peng Soon rarely made the first move, which Yifan put it down to his natural shyness. With one, she was diffident and reserved, and with the other, she was assertive and self-possessed. She often wondered if her nature had always allowed these opposites, this discrepancy of traits, and if not, why had it come so naturally to her? Yifan reasoned that she was not deceitful, no, only truthful to her own self, to her real desires—only human.

She lost her virginity to Hai Feng on the cusp of her 16th birthday, beside the river, near the fruit plantation where her parents worked. He had taken her there on the pretext of watching the sunset—the view offered a dreamy vista of the green-topped hills in the distance—and surprised her with a small chocolate cake and a plush teddy bear. She thanked him with a hug and a kiss, which led into a round of frantic fondling, to which Yifan offered no resistance. She was happy, and felt somewhat ready for what was to come, the next stage of their courtship.

She lay back on the dry stubbly ground and closed her eyes and listened to Hai Feng's soft grunts and the whispers of the nearby river. The pain came, as expected, but was not as bad as she had gathered from her classmates' stories; it was sharp for a few seconds, before dulling into a persistent, low-grade numbness. She had anticipated the hit of a rush, a build-up of sensations leading to something consequential—wasn't it supposed to lead to some feeling of pleasure? she thought—but all she felt was the clamminess and tightness in the lower half of her body, rigid and remote, cut off from the rest of her.

When Hai Feng was done—pulling out before he came copiously on her inner thigh—she quickly wiped herself off with a tissue, put on her panties and smoothed out her grass-stained skirt. Hai Feng immediately apologised, to which Yifan offered a consolatory smile and a pat on his back. They said nothing as they made their way back to Yifan's place in the somber twilight. After he dropped her off at her doorstep, Yifan left the cake in the fridge without touching it, and put the teddy bear with the rest of the soft toys on the bed she shared with her sisters. The panties she had worn, spotted with blood and dried-up cum, she disposed of by digging a hole in the field next to the house and burying it.

Three days later, while she was at Peng Soon's after school, she made love to him. They had to be quiet while they were at it, as Peng Soon's mother was at home, her footsteps audible even behind closed door. The attempt this time round went much better than her first, and Yifan was able to find a sliver of pleasure in what Peng Soon gave. While Hai Feng had rushed through the act, self-conscious and anxious to get to the end, Peng Soon was deliberate in his movements, slow and tentative, as if he were assessing every step of the lovemaking. Yifan looked up into his face as he entered her and started thrusting, his exertion visible with the lines of veins snaking up the sides of his neck. He took his time, and when he came, his body shook with a force that sent tendrils of shivers up Yifan's body. Before she left, he presented her with a birthday gift—of course, he had not forgotten. A watercolour of her face in close-up, rendered in light shades of yellow and pink, his initials scrawled in the right-hand corner. She kept it in a folder in the bottom drawer of her study table.

In the weeks after her 16th birthday, she had had sex with the two boys whenever she went out with them. It was what was on the boys' minds, the first and last thing they wanted when they leant in to press their bodies close to her, when they held her hands or kissed her. She could feel their urgency, and recognise her own; in meeting their needs, she was able to fulfil some of hers—her yearning for intimacy, for one. She could feel her body expanding under their touch, unfurling into new forms, yielding up new founts of pleasure, and there was an unquenchable, inexplicable delight to all of this.

Still, they had been careful; Yifan had insisted that the boys wear condoms, shortly after she had sex with them for the first time. But there had been several instances, in the heat and haste of the moment, where there had been lapses of judgement, a reckless abandonment of reason and precaution. It would be okay, they agreed, nothing bad would happen.

Yifan carried on her relationships with Hai Feng and Peng Soon for as long as she could, until one day, when she woke up feeling a terrible sickness in her guts and had to throw up in the toilet. The first time it happened, she did not think much of it, but when the frequency of the nausea and vomiting did not subside, she became alarmed.

Sensing something desperately amiss, Yifan bought a pregnancy test kit after school, and it confirmed all her doubts, made them concrete. She was surprised at how fast her luck had run out, at how promptly she had been dealt with a fate that she had no way to overcome.

Still, she refused to be shaken by the fact, though her mind threatened to spill over with a torrent of fears. She thought about the ways of handling the situation, and decided not to tell Hai Feng and Peng Soon about the pregnancy. What could they do if they knew? Their involvement would only complicate things, she reasoned. And so she kept everything to herself, even as her body bent itself to the changes taking place inside her.

In school, Yifan strove to remain her usual self, albeit now with greater self-awareness and even greater self-control, constantly aware that her body would betray her if she did not monitor herself with tight vigilance. So far no-one knew about her involvement with either of the boys; yes, some in her class knew she was close to Peng Soon, but assumed they were nothing more than just friends. And she had not let on about her relationship with Hai Feng, since theirs was a closeted courtship. Even if her schoolmates knew, they could not have guessed how far they had gone.

She kept herself sufficiently occupied with her studies and school assignments; yet, whenever she was alone, the doubts and anxiety would surface, leaving her breathless with helplessness. *Eat your sorrow,* she reminded herself.

As the weeks passed, Yifan lost her sense of self-mastery, succumbing more than usual to swinging moods of despondency and malaise. She avoided Hai Feng and Peng Soon. While they were worried and puzzled about her erratic behaviours, they could do absolutely nothing. She needed to put distance between herself and the boys, so as to get her thoughts in order, to think about her next steps.

At nights when she could not sleep, Yifan would flee into the humming forest and make her way to the river, her mind fired up by a sudden, irrational impulse. In the darkness around her, she sometimes imagined herself as a small nocturnal beast, feeling danger in the surroundings through its awakened senses, its thumping heartbeats pulsing through the edge of the skin. She saw herself through the eyes of this creature, a sad, pathetic sight. By the time she broke out of the cover of the forest, Yifan was no longer sure who or what she was—a creature prowling in the dark, or a figment of imagination conjured up by the forest. *If only, if it's possible,* she pleaded, *please, let me be someone else, something else.* She kept her gaze on the opposite bank of the river as her cries were swallowed by the fury of the passing currents, absolved and silenced. Wearied by her outburst, Yifan dropped to the ground and fell right into sleep, her body tucked in like a question mark.

One morning, sneaking back home after a night of dreamless sleep beside the river, Yifan came upon her mother standing by the back kitchen door. As she walked sheepishly towards her mother, averting her eyes, Yifan hoped to come up with an excuse—she was taking an early morning walk; she couldn't sleep—but something in her mother's forbidding posture cut her short. Yifan put her arms around her loose-fitting shirt, her stomach churning in sick, nauseous waves; she breathed in deeply to hold back the surge at the back of her throat. Her mother gripped her arm, as she walked past her.

What's going on? What have you done? she said, holding her arm firmly.

Yifan swiftly pulled away from her, but before she could take another step, she threw up at her mother's feet. The latter let out a cry and a sigh, putting her hand on Yifan's damp back, stroking it gently. Yifan, flinching from the touch, slipped away and scurried back to the bedroom, where her older sisters were slowly stirring awake. She did not get up that morning for school; she waited for the whole house to be quiet before she finally fell asleep.

In the afternoon, in the midst of a feverish recurring dream—she was always running in her dreams lately, heading somewhere or nowhere, she could never tell—she was woken up by a firm, insistent touch. Her mother, holding a bowl, telling her to sit up. Drink this, she said.

While Yifan was drinking the acrid concoction, her mother lifted her T-shirt and put her hand on Yifan's stomach. She glared at Yifan. *What were you thinking, you stupid girl?* her mother said, her voice low and strained. *Why did you go and ruin your life? You stupid, foolish girl.*

Yifan pushed her mother's hand aside and slipped back under the blanket, the bitterness on her mouth working its way into her guts. There was no way to hide it now, she thought, she had to find her own way out of this.

That night, knowing full well that her mother would press her for the only thing she wanted to know—*whose was it?*—Yifan told her the full story, one she had started fabricating since the knowledge of her pregnancy. She did not want to involve Hai Feng and Peng Soon in this, especially since there was no way she could tell which of them was the father. So she came up with a story she hoped would invite the least suspicion. A man, a stranger, had appeared out of nowhere while she walking home along the forest path one afternoon, and dragged her to a secluded spot behind a thick brush and raped her. It happened three months or so ago, and she did not dare to tell anymore, Yifan said, her voice quavering in the telling.

When her mother placed her hand on hers, Yifan broke into tears. *I didn't know what to do,* she said mournfully.

We need to report this, her mother said.

No, no, Yifan insisted, *I can't, let's not.* Her mother shook her head, her eyes heavy with sorrow. *And please don't tell Papa, he'll kill me.*

Having told this story to her mother and swearing her to secrecy, Yifan did not feel any better. She knew she could have told her mother the truth, but the truth wasn't something that had felt right or appropriate at the moment. It was enough that she alone knew what she had done—frankly, did it matter to anyone else?—and that she would be able to live with it somehow. She would have to manage the consequences, no matter the cost. She only needed to get through it one step at a time.

Two days later, on a Thursday, her mother told her to skip school; she was taking her to see someone. Yifan, sensing her mother's silent disapprobation, did not ask any questions, and did as she was told.

They took a bus from the city centre to a town an

hour away. They did not speak on the ride there; Yifan stared out of the window the whole time, the landscape flitting by in an endless, sandy blur. When the bus hit a pothole, she felt the tiniest of movements in her stomach. Had she really felt it? Or had she just imagined it? Even now, she refused to acknowledge that whatever was inside her was something alive or real. She absolutely refused to give it a definite form in her mind, or even call it a baby: such an ugly, ill-formed word. Gripping her hands in her lap, Yifan did not dare to go any further with the thought.

They alighted along a row of old shophouses, and her mother, in a brief moment of uncertainty, looked up and down the quiet street, checking the signs. Then she started walking down one of the back alleys, and Yifan followed close behind. They turned into an entryway beside a bakery and climbed up a narrow staircase.

Her mother knocked on one of the doors along the corridor, and the long, pale face of a matronly woman popped into view. They were quickly ushered in, the woman's head and her mother's bent solemnly in a whispered conversation. The old woman took a few glances at Yifan, her expression impassive, unreadable. While they talked, Yifan sat on a wooden stool and stared at her fingers. She knew what was coming and told herself not to panic, and not to give in to her fears. She drilled her mother's words into herself, an incantation: *eat your sorrow*. It had to be done, and it would be over soon. It was for her own good.

Her mother returned to her side and sat with her for a long, quiet moment, not looking at her. The old woman came out of a side room wearing an off-white coat, and called out to Yifan. She rose and entered the dim dusty room and lay on a thin bed with cool, soft sheets and waited for instructions. When she felt the cold probe entering her, spreading the folds between her legs, Yifan closed her eyes and let her mind slip into a daydream.

In it, she was back at the river, half asleep, listening to the rippling of the water. She sensed a presence emerging from the void of the night, out of the forest. It moved with the silence and stealth of an animal that was used to the dark. She did not raise her eyes to it or make any moves. The creature came right to her feet, radiating heat from its body, breathing hotly on her skin. Yifan kept very still, anticipating the sharp snap of jaws or fangs, but instead all she felt was a sandpapery tongue licking at her soles and moving up her legs. Her body shivered with an unbridled force, as if she were trying to break out of the shroud of her own body. She spread her legs, and the creature stuck its rough tongue into her and extended its full length inside her. Yifan gasped in agony, plummeting right into an oblivion deeper than death.

When it was finally over, Yifan felt as if the different parts of her body had become disassociated, forcibly stitched together into a person. She stepped out of the room depleted, a wisp of chaff in the shell of her new body.

She returned to school the following week. In the days that ensued, she felt nothing but the faintest impressions from the things and people around her, as if everything were coming to her from a great and vast distance, vague and impenetrable. She moved through the days like a spectre passing through invisible walls of time, neither here nor there. The voices and laughter and noisy chatter of her classmates were a language that had slipped from her tongue; how would she ever learn to speak it again? She had been exiled, a refugee with no status.

It was during this period of time that she started cutting herself to feel something, anything. A cut was all it took to feel a different kind of pain: quick, sharp and bracing—one removed from the dull, constant, unswerving pain she had been feeling since that day she stepped out of the old woman's room.

Yifan had refused to see Hai Feng or Peng Soon while she was recuperating at home; her mother told everyone she had a bout of stomach flu. When Hai Feng came up to her during recess on her first day back in school, Yifan smiled and steeled herself to the slew of questions. But when he reached out to touch her hand, Yifan flinched.

What's wrong? he asked.

I'm still not feeling well, that's all, she said, before turning to walk away.

In class, Peng Soon left small notes on her desk, which she crumpled without reading. When he turned to glance at her, attempting to get her attention, Yifan ignored him by staring rigidly ahead at the teacher or the chalkboard. When school ended, Yifan was among the first at the gates, making a quick exit.

By the end of the third week, Yifan could no longer find the strength to keep up appearances. The walls of her mind had finally caved in; everything seemed intolerable, beyond her. She stayed in bed the whole day, drifting in and out of sleep, mumbling to herself. Her mother came to her in the evening and, after taking a long assessment of Yifan's condition, began to make the necessary plans with a few phone calls. Yifan was to be sent to stay with her aunt, her mother's younger sister, and her family in Skudai, Johor Bahru, for a period of time.

Within two days, Yifan was on the bus, a small suitcase

by her side. She left on the first bus out of Ipoh, the day still steeped in veiled darkness. At her aunt's, Yifan settled quickly into a semblance of a life, helping her aunt and uncle at their bak kut teh stall instead of furthering her studies. Her past was an old story she had put behind her, quickly forgotten, worthless.

While Yifan continued to keep in touch with her mother and sisters with occasional phone calls and letters, she did not return to Ipoh, not even when her father died three years later of lung cancer. When the opportunity to work in Singapore presented itself through one of her aunt's contacts, Yifan took it up immediately, ready to make something new out of a life she had slowly pieced together.

And what was her life, really, but the stories she made out of it? Time and again Yifan told herself stories she sincerely and wholeheartedly believed to be as close to the truth as she could possibly make of her fragmented history. The past was gone; the stories of it could still be reinvented, retold, over and over again.

• • •

As she collected her thoughts about the past and put them away in her mind, Yifan tucked the photograph back into the album and turned her mind to other matters. She needed to unpack her suitcase and settle into a new life here in Ipoh. Over a dinner of stir-fried petai with garlic and anchovies and steamed batang fish, Yifan and her mother chatted lightly about news and gossip concerning relatives and old neighbours. Yifan was glad that her mother did not bring up the question of her return. Perhaps in a day or two, after she had settled in, she would have to tell her. Living alone for the two years after the last of her siblings moved out had deepened the traits of stillness and stoicism that were always apparent in her mother. In her calm presence, Yifan could feel her own mind quietening down, smoothing over. Still, she could not ignore the signs of her mother's physical decline: her dwindling, hunched frame, the blue-ringed irises, the deep creases on her face. In Yifan's mind, her mother had in some ways seemed indefatigable, sturdy and resolute in her being and demeanour; in others, she came across as utterly fragile, worn-out and alone.

After dinner, Yifan decided to take a walk. She had not been sure whether she still remembered the route to the river, but once she was on the path, muscle memory took over, directing her down several bends among the trees. The air was cooler now, and her mind was alert to the mounting murmurs of the night. The forest had thickened in many parts, reaching out to scratch Yifan on her calves and arms. From a distance, she could hear the soft gush of the river; shortly after she caught sight of the shimmering band of light and motion. Stepping into the moonlit clearing, Yifan let out a deep sigh, the air around her surprisingly bracing. She put a hand on her stomach, anticipating subtle movements, but it was still in the early phases, and any movement she might have felt was probably imagined.

It was only a fortnight ago when she had tested herself with a pregnancy kit and confirmed what she already knew. The early signs had been unmistakable: a missed period, the slight swelling of her breasts, the constant nausea. The knowledge of the pregnancy brought with it a reawakening of an old, almost-forgotten dread—cold fingers of fear creeping up the inside of her calves, coring her hollow. The dusty, sun-dappled room, the rich, metallic reek of her blood, the old now-faceless woman. The baby, her baby—no, it wasn't hers, not at all, Yifan pushed away the thought—plucked, taken away.

She shuddered uncontrollably; her body remembered the old wounds, its deepest loss. Much as she wished things were different this time round, with different circumstances, it was unfortunately not the case. She was where she was, eight years ago, with an unplanned pregnancy, and a heart riddled and sickened with indecision and crippling dread. As she stood by the river, Yifan let her mind slip, unguarded, into thoughts of Derrick and Tien Chen.

She had met Derrick at a newly-opened gelato café her flatmate had brought her to. She had been standing behind him in the queue; he had turned to her and suggested the D24 durian flavour, if she wasn't turned off by the taste of the fruit. She had smiled politely, and Derrick had taken the lead with a run of questions.

She had liked Derrick there and then, with his charming lopsided smile and easy, offhand manner that was at once self-assured and affecting. Yifan had only been working in Singapore for five months then, at a seafood restaurant along Upper Thomson Road, and was feeling slightly adrift, lonely. She didn't need much persuasion to take up the offer of a coffee date with Derrick—she needed to broaden her social circle, which at that point was made up entirely of her Malaysian flatmates.

From their dates, she gathered that Derrick was a writer of short stories, and had five published collections. Though she wasn't much of a reader, she borrowed one of his books from the library out of curiosity. Most of the stories were simple enough to understand, and while she would have liked to talk about some of them with him, she didn't.

Given her lack of knowledge about literature, she didn't know how or what to begin with. In any case, Derrick rarely talked about his writing, though Yifan knew he put in long hours into it, writing late into the night, sacrificing sleep and health. He was often distracted if he was working on a new story, something he dismissed as general tiredness, which Yifan chided him gently for.

The first time she spent the night over at his place, Yifan had gone around his flat while he was sleeping, looking at the books on the shelves, and reading printouts of a new story that he had put on his table. There were lines of crossed-out text as well as scribblings in pencil on the sides of the pages. As she read the story, Yifan could not help reading the marginalia, too. She made sure to leave things as they were, careful not to leave behind any telltale tracks.

By the time a few weeks passed Yifan had learnt that, apart from his writing, there was not much in life that held his interest or that he cared for. He had a small group of acquaintances, classmates from university, but he was not close to them. As for his family, Derrick revealed very little, only mentioning in passing the deaths of his parents six months apart, and an estranged relationship with an older brother.

Still, the early months of her relationship with Derrick were a heady period of small pleasures and simple gratification.

Yifan had sunk into it with a hunger that had caught her by surprise. She was madly in love, and every possibility seemed open to her then. For once she dared to imagine a future for herself, something permanent and within reach. Of course, she was aware of Derrick's faults—his frequent mood swings, his aloofness, the long unexpected bouts of his depression—but they had felt minor and manageable in the larger view of things. Yifan was sure he could change if she helped him along.

It was two months into the relationship before Yifan found out about Derrick's on-off drug use. He was quick to assure her it was only a casual habit, nothing serious, that he had it under control. Only Special K, XTC, ice—not the hard stuff, definitely not heroin, he told her. And she believed him for a while, before witnessing a series of blackouts that broke the faith she had in him.

Not wanting to be pulled deeper into a relationship that felt like it had already run its full course, Yifan decided to break up with Derrick. She was surprised when he let the whole thing slip away quietly and undemonstratively, with barely any reaction—no remorse, no guilt. He proceeded to shut her out of his life completely, refusing to pick up her calls or return her text messages, as if she had been nothing but a passing fancy, a one-time fling. It had hurt her to know that the relationship had mattered more to her than him, that whatever love she had felt was merely a fantasy she had conjured up. She felt foolish and chastened.

For some time after the breakup, Yifan did not go out with anyone, a deliberate choice on her part. She took up longer shifts at the seafood restaurant where she worked six days a week. On her day off she would stay in the flat and catch up on TVB and Korean drama serials. When her flatmates wanted to set up dates for her, she declined civilly, diverting their attention elsewhere. She would have preferred to live by herself, or at least have her own room, but her salary was barely enough to cover rent and basic necessities. She had considered other job options, which were few and far between, given her lack of paper qualifications. Even the idea of being a beer promoter held a certain appeal to her at one point; it paid the same amount as her current job, but with fewer hours and more flexible work arrangements. But she had seen the stares that were levelled at these beer promoters at the kopitiam, and it was something she didn't feel comfortable about.

Sometimes she looked at her flatmates who held down office jobs, as secretaries or human resource assistants or sales associates, and wondered what her life could have been if she had stayed in Ipoh and completed her studies. What direction would her life have taken then? Would it have been better? She would break the train of such thoughts with a shake of her head. It would do no good to be plagued by the possibilities of a life she had never lived. She narrowed her vision and kept her anxiety in check. All she needed to do was to work hard and save whatever she could, and who knew? Her life might take a turn for the better.

It was in this period of time, where she had resolved to keep her nose to the grindstone and turn her life around, that Yifan got to know Tien Chen. She had quit her job at the seafood restaurant after a nasty fallout with another waitress, and was working at a zi-char stall in a kopitiam. After her disastrous relationship with Derrick, she was wary of starting something new, and did little to encourage his attention. But he returned to the kopitiam every night and made every effort to talk to her.

Still, she continued to hold back—she wasn't quite ready yet. While Tien Chen was persistent in his advances, he was not pushy, which allowed Yifan sufficient time to assess him. When she talked to him, Yifan was often reminded of Peng Soon—his natural reticence, an observant eye that took in the smallest details, his pale, veiny hands. It was a reminder that would have pained her, if the bite of the recollection hadn't long faded. Whenever Tien Chen leant in to listen to her, Yifan had the uncanny sense that he was trying to commit everything she said to memory, as if every word were something he was using to build an image of her in his head, an effigy upon which he could invest his own emotions, to stake his claim.

She took the leap eventually, and her decision was justly rewarded: Tien Chen returned her affections with a fervency that dwarfed hers in every aspect. Whenever they went out on dates, he took up her suggestions willingly, and was quick to read and respond to her every mood. Yet, despite his easy, tractable nature, Yifan still felt a tiny chill of fear, an animal instinct cultivated from past experiences: how much of this was real, and would it truly last? While she had told him all that she was willing to reveal about her past, there were still many things she had left in the dark; and if so, how could he really know her for who she was? And for all she knew about him, she might know very little as well, for even though Tien Chen was patently straightforward and complaisant, there was an opaqueness to him that Yifan could not quite put a finger on.

Yifan wondered if knowing every part of him was necessary to love him fully. How does love work, she thought—with full disclosure, or certain blindness? For every attempt she had made at love—with Hai Feng, Peng Soon, and

Derrick—there was always something she found wanting. Did the fault lie with her—in her ignorance, her duplicity, her own omission? Had she always been the one to make a mess of things? With Tien Chen, she felt like she had been given yet another chance to make it right, to redeem herself.

Things would have gone well between her and Tien Chen, had it not been for that chance encounter with Derrick at the hospital three months ago; she had been there to visit a flatmate who was hospitalised after a surgery to treat appendicitis. She had seen him at the pharmacy and contemplated whether to make the first contact. She noticed the bandage on his left wrist, and noted a dull languidness in his movements, a blankness in his eyes. There was something broken and helpless in Derrick's demeanour that spoke to Yifan. So she made her decision and called out his name, presenting a different side of her to him —a more measured, charitable self. She had once again slipped into an old familiar role, effortlessly, as if it had always been there, lying dormant in the core of who she was.

When Yifan first reached out to Derrick, she had only wanted to offer some comfort, a little kindness. But she soon found herself caught in a tangle of feelings for him, a rekindling of old affections, even as she tried to suppress them. This time he truly needed her, and because it was a need that she could understand and meet, she gave what she could. She was only helping him to get back on his feet, she told herself. When he recovered, she would leave.

Yifan sensed the pull of something dark inside him, ready to tip him into its chasm again, so to distract him from whatever lurked within him, to offer him a way to get out of his own head, she asked him to read her his stories. In return she told him the story of the fox spirit. As she told it over the nights, it began to feel like a real but forgotten part of her past, and she fell right into its hold, believing it fully and unreservedly, as if she had truly lived every part of it.

Before long, Yifan was moving between the two men, between the different selves she was inhabiting, living out an existence that had felt familiar and precarious. How had it come to this—her history turning around, biting its own tail? Had she failed, once again, in a test to prove herself better than her actions? Every choice she had made—to love Tien Chen, to take care of Derrick—was made in good, clear conscience, but still the outcome was the same, every good intention gone to seed. At times, Yifan could not shake off the dread that at any moment everything would implode.

And then it did, and again she was on the lam, trying to outrun the consequences. But how far could she run this time?

Yifan closed her eyes and took a deep breath of the cold night air. The forest pressed itself against her, whispering into her ears. All her senses felt raw and tender. *Time to head back,* she told herself, *you're tired, it's been a long day.* The river pushed its way through the darkness into her. She stood there for a while longer, falling and falling.

• • •

Tossed out of a half-remembered dream (how vivid it was, the water on her skin, the breathlessness of full submission), Yifan sat up on the bed, her T-shirt damp on her back, her mind already kicking into full consciousness. The coy bluish light of dawn had crept into the bedroom, barely illuminating the dusty corners. The dream was one she'd had before: she recalled a good part of it as she stared out into the grassy courtyard. She felt herself refreshed by the memory, comforted. From the depth of the house, Yifan could hear the sounds of cooking and her mother moving about. Quietly, she slipped out of bed and went over to the window. Mornings were her favourite part of the day: the riot of colours breaking up the grey sky, the lightness of the dewy air, and the stark, solitary beauty in everything—a tree, a blade of grass, a still-darkened house. Yifan had always been an early riser, and she had woken at this hour for the past week, her body already attuned to a certain rhythm. With little fuss, her days had fallen into a fixed, narrow pattern: house chores after breakfast, long walks around the town in the afternoon, meals with her mother, TV-watching at night.

On one of her walks, she had visited her old secondary school and stood at the rusty gates, looking in at the students in the compound; she could not recognise any of the teachers, or spot the casuarina tree where she had spent her recesses with Peng Soon. From what she had heard from her mother, Peng Soon was now a teacher.

In the old school? she had asked.

No, in Kuala Lumpur, in an international school, her mother said.

She had not asked about Hai Feng. The provision shop was still there, at the junction leading out of the kampung. She had peeked into it a few times and seen a short, middle-aged man standing behind the glass counter. Was it Hai Feng's father? She would sneak away just as the man looked up and noticed her, raising his black thick-rimmed spectacles.

Sometimes, sitting at a roadside food stall, Yifan would glance at a face, finding it familiar, and wonder whether it was someone she knew back in school. She waited for the moment of recognition, which unfortunately never came, before turning away.

A soft knock on the door: her mother's voice, alerting her to breakfast. Yifan removed a face towel from the rack and started her day.

In the kitchen, her mother had laid out breakfast: mugs of coffee sweetened with condensed milk, steamed red bean buns, a plate of bee hoon. Yifan sipped the hot Milo; her appetite had been erratic since her return, dormant at times, occasionally flaring into irrational spates of cravings: pork ribs soup, mee rebus, fried oyster omelette.

Eat, eat, while it's hot, her mother said, pushing the plate of steamed buns towards her. Yifan picked one up and nibbled at the edge.

What are your plans today? her mother asked.

Nothing, the same, I guess, just walk around, Yifan said. They ate in silence.

Later, while they were washing the dishes at the concrete wash trough, her mother said: *You can tell me if you have problems.* A pause. Then she added: *Stay as long as you like. Don't be in a hurry to leave.* Yifan nodded, and moved away from her mother.

That afternoon, as Yifan came back from her walk in a different part of town, where the old fruit plantations used to be, her mother hurried out of the house, a look of fazed concern on her face. *There's someone who was looking for you*, she said. *I told him you're out, and he said he will come back later.*

Who? Yifan asked.

He told me his name, but I can't remember now. A tall guy, with spectacles. He looks quite pleasant.

Yifan tried, and failed, to keep her face neutral. A look of alarm must have crawled onto her features, which clouded her mother's in turn. *Where did he go?* she asked.

Not sure, maybe somewhere nearby, I told him you'll be back soon.

Yifan quickly found an excuse to escape into her room. Sitting on the bed, she suddenly found it hard to breathe. She got up and started pacing the shrinking room, her mind stubbornly vacant except for a single overriding thought: *Go, leave now.* There was still a narrow opening to leave all this behind.

Yifan opened the bedroom door, slipped down the corridor, and left through the back entrance to the kitchen. Sunlight poured from the open sky, and the lusty chirping of crickets filled the hot, stifling air. At Yifan's approach, a brood of chickens burst into short manic leaps of flight, scattering in different directions.

Moving with a steady pace along the hardened path, Yifan emerged from the cool, grey canopy of the forest into the clearing, her vision momentarily overwhelmed by sunlight. In the day, the river brimmed with unrestrained life, glistening with sheets of bright hard scales. Peering into the water, Yifan could see the sandy bottom, soft and brown, dappled by flashing gems of light and shadow. She would not go any further, she knew. She sat down in the shade of the nearest tree, looking out to the hills in the distance.

She would have to wait now. For something to happen—but what? What did she know? What had she understood of the choices she'd made? For all the different lives she had lived and the countless stories she had told, there had never been a point where she had felt fully understood by anyone. She would be present as one of her many selves, playing a role in a story of her making. And yet she remained almost invisible, barely grasped by the men who loved her, those who strove to lay their claims on her. Who was she to them exactly—and did they ever really, truly, know her? What had they seen in her, this woman made in their own estimation, moulded out of the bits and fragments she had allowed them to know? A thing of many forms and many faces, perhaps? And, if so, who had they really loved then—which Yifan had they fallen in love with?

And, in the end, did their love matter at all?

From a distance, a voice called out a name. Yifan heard it. But she did not turn to find out where it was coming from. The name came again, louder, insistent. A presence now—a figure standing in the clearing—heavy, physical, singular, coming closer, hovering next to her.

Yifan closed her eyes, and took a long breath.

Life, again, touching.

ACKNOWLEDGEMENTS

Endless gratitude and thanks to the following people:
My family: Pa, Ma, Siew Yen, Harry, Thiam Teck and Agustiniwati. Literally for everything, every single thing.

My four brave and beautiful foxes: Ryan, Gabriel, Kristine, Gareth. Go wild, roam free, explore, discover, you little beasts!

My friends: Kok Wei, Jenny, Yew Pin, Angeline, Alvin, Fiona, Gavin Ng, Yvonne Lee, Eric Soo. For sustaining me in spirit and kindness over the long years.

Jocelyn Lau: for reading earlier drafts and providing invaluable feedback.

The lovely folks at Epigram Books: Edmund for his steadfast belief, Jason Erik Lundberg for his generous support and guidance, and JY Yang for saving the book, word by word (you're a godsend! I owe you big). Also, a hearty nod to Winston and Andy for their hard work, and to Qin Yi for the gorgeous book cover.

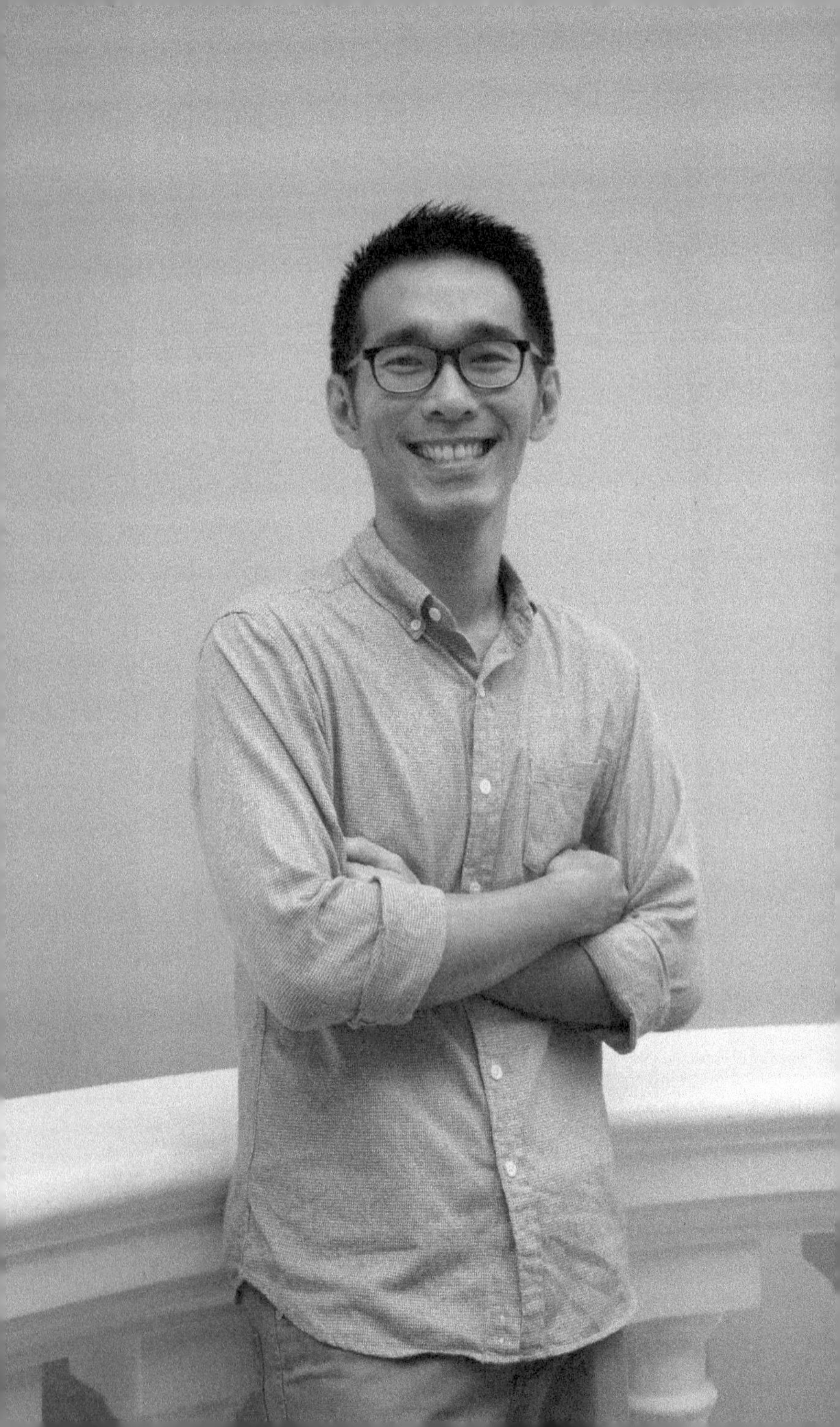

ABOUT THE AUTHOR

O Thiam Chin is the winner of the inaugural Epigram Books Fiction Prize in 2015, for his first novel, *Now That's It's Over*. He is also the author of five collections of short fiction: *Free-Falling Man* (2006), *Never Been Better* (2009), *Under the Sun* (2010), *The Rest of Your Life and Everything That Comes With It* (2011) and *Love, Or Something Like Love* (2013, shortlisted for the 2014 Singapore Literature Prize for English Fiction).

His short stories have appeared in *Mānoa, World Literature Today, The International Literary Quarterly, Asia Literary Review, Quarterly Literary Review Singapore, Cha: An Asian Literary Journal, Kyoto Journal, The Jakarta Post, The New Straits Times, Asiatic and Esquire (Singapore)*. His short fiction was also selected for the first two volumes of the *Best New Singaporean Short Stories* anthology series.

O was an honorary fellow of the Iowa International Writing Program in 2010, a recipient of the NAC Young Artist Award in 2012, and has been thrice longlisted for the Frank O'Connor International Short Story Award. He appears frequently at writers festivals in Australia, Indonesia and Singapore.

Once We Were There
BERNICE CHAULY

Journalist Delonix Regia chances upon the cultured and irresistible Omar amidst the upheaval of the Reformasi movement in Kuala Lumpur. As the city roils around them, they find solace in love, marriage, and then parenthood. But when their two-year-old daughter Alba is kidnapped, Del must confront the terrible secret of a city where babies are sold and girls trafficked. By turns heartbreaking and suspenseful, *Once We Were There* is a debut novel of profound insight. It is Bernice Chauly at her very best.

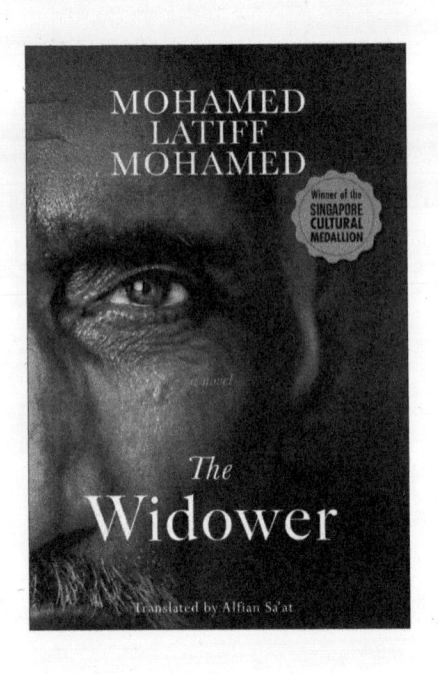

The Widower
MOHAMED LATIFF MOHAMED

Former political detainee and professor Pak Karman loses his wife in a car accident. The intensity of his mourning causes him to become untethered from his sanity. As reality, memory and fantasy become more and more blurred, he must come to terms with his past actions before his grief overwhelms him completely. Mohamed's novel, hailed as a landmark in modernist Malay fiction, is an unsettling tale of psychic disintegration and obsessive love.

The Tower
ISA KAMARI

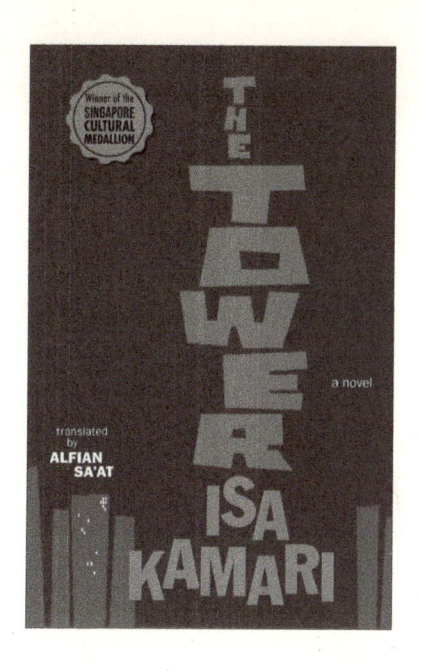

A masterful tale of success and failure. A successful architect visits the new skyscraper he designed. As he climbs the tower with Ilham, his clerk of works, he reflects upon his life and spiritual journey in an increasingly materialistic world. As he struggles to reach the top, he is plagued by memories of a dark past. These memories are woven through the narrative as a series of fables and elliptical digressions, mirroring his own increasingly fractured state of mind.

State of Emergency
JEREMY THIAM

A woman finds herself questioned for a conspiracy she did not take part in. A son flees to London to escape from a father, wracked by betrayal. A journalist seeks to uncover the truth of the place she once called home. A young wife leaves her husband and children behind to fight for freedom in the jungles of Malaya. *State of Emergency* traces the leftist movements of Singapore and Malaysia from the 1940s to the present day, centring on a family trying to navigate the choppy political currents of the region.

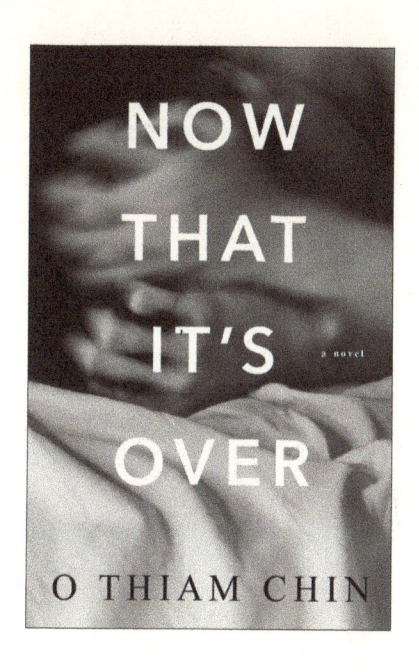

Now That It's Over
O THIAM CHIN

During the Christmas holidays in 2004, an earthquake in the Indian Ocean triggers a tsunami that devastates fourteen countries. Two couples from Singapore are vacationing in Phuket when the tsunami strikes. Alternating between the aftermath of the catastrophe and past events that led these characters to that fateful moment, *Now That It's Over* weaves a tapestry of causality and regret, and chronicles the physical and emotional wreckage wrought by natural and man-made disasters.

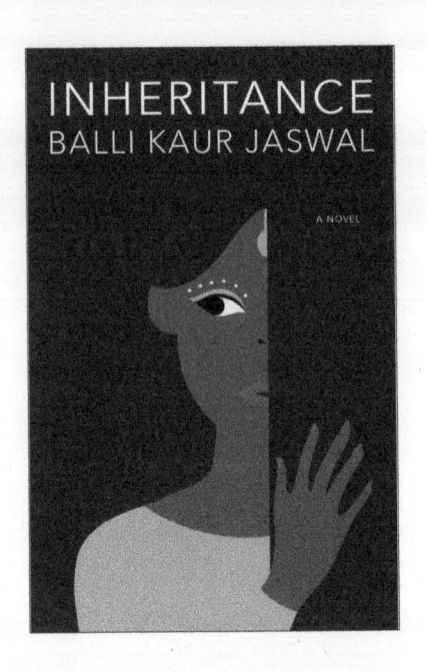

Inheritance
BALLI KAUR JASWAL

In 1971, a teenage girl briefly disappears from her house in the middle of the night, only to return a different person, causing fissures that threaten to fracture her Punjabi Sikh family. As Singapore's political and social landscapes evolve, the family must cope with shifting attitudes towards castes, youth culture, sex and gender roles, identity and belonging. Inheritance examines each family member's struggles to either preserve or buck tradition in the face of a changing nation.